It was like being hit with an iron fist

Dominic wanted her!

Christy opened her mouth and closed it again and then heard him say in a thick, unfamiliar tone, "Do that again."

She offered her lips instinctively to absorb the heat of his as he pulled her against him and kissed her with a famished kind of hunger.

Against her mouth she heard him mutter, "You can't know how much I've wanted to do this. I want you, Christy. I want to make love to you."

It was his voice that brought her back to reality. She pushed him away, shaking her head, and as she did so she saw him frown as bitterness crept into his eyes. "You'll have to forgive me. I forgot that you were committed elsewhere."

PENNY JORDAN was constantly in trouble in school because of her inability to stop daydreaming—especially during French lessons. In her teens she was an avid romance reader, although it didn't occur to her to try writing one herself until she was older. "My first half-dozen attempts ended up ingloriously," she remembers, "but I persevered, and one manuscript was finished." She plucked up the courage to send it to a publisher, convinced her book would be rejected. It wasn't, and the rest is history! Penny is married and lives in Cheshire.

Books by Penny Jordan

HARLEQUIN PRESENTS

HARLEQUIN SIGNATURE EDITION

PENNY JORDAN

a savage adoration

Harlequin Books

TORONTO • NEW YORK • LONDON
AMSTERDAM • PARIS • SYDNEY • HAMBURG
STOCKHOLM • ATHENS • TOKYO • MILAN

Harlequin Presents first edition March 1988
ISBN 0-373-11057-X

Original hardcover edition published in 1987
by Mills & Boon Limited

CHAPTER ONE

CHRISTY opened the kitchen door and stepped out into the garden. The air smelled of snow. She breathed it in slowly, savouring the crisp scent of it, and looked at the leaden winter sky.

A thin curl of smoke from her father's bonfire smudged the skyline before mingling with the greyness of the cloud. Beyond the garden lay a vista of fields broken by clumps of woodland, backed by the slopes of the Border hills, their peaks already whitened by the first fall of snow. Everything lay intensely still beneath the cold January air. It was all so very different from London and the life she had lived there, but it was familiar as well. After all, she had spent the first seventeen years of her life in these Border hills. And the last eight away from them, apart from brief visits home.

She reached the bottom of the garden and stood for a moment watching her father as he threw the last of the rubbish on his bonfire. He was wearing the same tweeds she remembered from her teenage years, shabby and well worn. He turned and saw her, and smiled affectionately at her; a tall, mild-mannered man who had passed on to her, his only child, his height.

'Lunch is ready,' she told him.

'Good, I'm hungry. I'll just damp this fire down and then I'll be in.'

If her height had come from her father, then her oval green eyes had come from her mother's Celtic ancestors, like her rich banner of copper hair, and her quick temper. Scots and English had quarrelled and married across the Border for centuries, but her mother's family had been Highlanders from Glen Coe, and she had often bemoaned the fact that Christy seemed to have inherited their fierce warring spirit.

Christy waited for her father to finish putting out the fire.

'You know, Christy,' he said, 'it's good to have you home, although I wish it could have been in happier circumstances. You don't have to stay, you know. Your mother . . .'

'I *want* to stay,' she interrupted firmly. 'I would have come home even if Mum hadn't had to have that operation. You know, in London it's all too easy to get out of touch with reality, with everything that's important in life.' She sighed faintly, a frown touching her smooth forehead. 'I've given up my job, Dad.'

There hadn't been time in the frantic telephone call telling her of her mother's emergency operation for Christy to tell her father her own news, but now that the danger was over and her mother was safely back at home, it was time for her to talk of her own plans.

Now it was her father's turn to frown, and Christy looked away from him. She could sense his surprise and concern, and bit down hard on her bottom lip.

'But you seemed so pleased to be working for David Galvin,' he said. 'When you came home last summer you seemed so happy.'

'I was. But David has been asked to write the music for a film and to do that he has to go out to Hollywood.

He asked me to go with him, but I didn't want to, so I handed in my notice.'

She prayed that her father would accept her explanation at face value and not press her any closer. What she had told him was in effect the truth, but there was a great deal that she had concealed from him.

There was David's desire for them to become lovers, for a start. She shivered slightly, a frisson of sensation running through her that had nothing to do with the cold. She didn't love David, but he was a very magnetic and masculine man; she had known that if he continued to press her she might have been very tempted to give in to him—and how she would have hated herself if she had done so. She wasn't blind, or a fool; she knew that David was almost consistently unfaithful to his wife Meryl, and that Meryl accepted his infidelities as the price of being married to a man whose artistic abilities had made him world-famous by the time he was thirty years old.

The sort of affairs David indulged in meant nothing in any emotional sense; he was an intensely sensual and sexual man who enjoyed women and, shamingly, she knew that there had been the odd moment when she had not been sure of her own ability to withstand him should he choose to use the full force of his sexual power against her.

She had worked for him for four years, and had been accepted by Meryl and his children almost as an honorary member of the family. She knew what his brief affairs did to them, and the last thing she wanted was to inflict further hurt on them, so she had done the only thing possible: she had run away.

He had flung that at her in their final confrontation. She had told him just before Christmas that she was resigning. There had been no need for him to ask why, and she remembered how his mouth had compressed with anger and mockery. There was an almost childish side to him that loathed being thwarted or denied anything he had set his heart on, and he *had* wanted her. Consequently he had used that skilful tongue of his mercilessly to destroy her defences, bringing her close to the edge of tears and total self-betrayal, but somehow she had managed to hang on to her self-control. A small, bitter smile twisted her mouth. She knew whom she had to thank for that self-control, for that hard-won ability to refuse to give in to her feelings. It seemed that she was doomed to be unlucky in the men in her life.

She had spent Christmas alone, refusing Meryl's pleas to join them in their huge Wimbledon house, as she had done at other Christmases, and then, just when she had felt that her loneliness and misery might cause her to give way, she had received a telephone call from her father telling her of her mother's collapse.

She hadn't wasted a moment in racing home, and now that she was here she intended to stay. She felt calmer, safer, more secure than she had felt in a long time. Her mother was going to need careful looking after for at least a couple of months—plenty of time for her to think about what she was going to do with the rest of her life. She could even work for her father in his busy country solicitor's practice if need be; his secretary of thirty years was on the point of retiring. She knew she had made the right decision; the *only* decision. If she had stayed in London, David might have found a way of persuading her to go to Hollywood with him after all, ostensibly as his personal assistant, of course . . . but she had known that her agreement to go would have been her agreement to their affair.

So, instead, she had ruthlessly cut all her links with London, giving up her flat and her few friends. It had been disturbing to realise how few friends she had to show for eight years in London, but then she had always been something of a loner, cautious about revealing or giving anything of herself, and even more so after that disastrous summer when she was seventeen.

Her mouth compressed again as she opened the back door and went into the warm kitchen.

Her parents' home stood almost alone at the end of a narrow country lane, some ten miles outside the town where her father practised. They had come here shortly after their marriage, when her father had bought himself into the partnership. Now the other partners were either dead or retired, and her father ran the business alone with the help of a young articled clerk.

The house was solidly built of local stone, sheltered from the harsh winters that could affect the Borders by the small valley in which it stood. The village, with its school and church, was less than a mile away, and Christy could vividly remember the long winter trudges through the snow to the village bus stop, where as a teenager she had waited with the other children for the bus to take them to school. Those had been good days; life had been simple then, and she had been happy, if somewhat alone. The other children had often teased her, calling her 'Carrots' because of her red hair.

What was past was past, she reminded herself as she dished up the lunch. She had already been up to see her mother and supervise the very light meal that was all she was allowed at present.

'I had a message from the surgery this morning to say that the doctor would be out to see Mother this afternoon. Do you still have Doctor Broughton?' she asked her father as he sat down.

'No. Didn't your mother tell you? Alan Broughton retired early just before Christmas. Dominic Savage is our doctor now.'

Christy's arm jerked and she spilled some carrots. She was glad that she was facing the Aga and that her father couldn't see her expression.

'Dominic? I thought he was in America?'

'So he was, but he decided to come back. I suppose it's only natural in a way. His grandfather was the only GP here for a long time, and he was responsible for starting up our present practice.'

'But Dominic always seemed so ... so ambitious ...'

'People change.' Her father smiled, and there was a slight twinkle in his eye. 'Look at you, for instance. I seem to remember a time when we couldn't mention Dominic's name without you colouring up like a sunset.'

She fought down the panic and pain clawing through her stomach and summoned a brief smile.

'Yes, I was rather obvious in my adolescent adoration, wasn't I? Thank goodness we all grow out of that sort of thing! I must have driven you all mad, especially Dominic . . .'

'Oh, I don't know. It always seemed to me that he had rather a soft spot for you.'

A soft spot! If only her father knew. The last thing she had expected or wanted when she came running for home and safety had been to meet up with Dominic Savage again—the very last thing. She doubted her ability to face him with equanimity and coolness even at her most self-composed, but having to face him like this, when she was feeling so vulnerable and torn . . . She shuddered slightly, remembering how his cold grey eyes could see through her defences, and how that deep incisive voice of his could shred through her puny arguments.

Her heart was pounding as she served the rest of the meal. If she could have, she would have got on the next train to London and stayed there, but it was too late, she had burned her bridges, and then there were her parents to consider. Her mother needed careful looking after—someone to watch over her and make sure that she didn't do too much. Christy knew her mother; she had always led an active, busy life, and she wouldn't take kindly to her restricted regime.

Dominic Savage back in Setondale; that was the last thing she had expected, or wanted.

While she cleared away after their meal, her father went upstairs to sit with her mother. Dominic was due at three o'clock, and Christy wondered cravenly if she could find some excuse not to be there when he called. Her face burned as she remembered their last horrific meeting.

It was true that at seventeen she had had a

mammoth crush on him; but what her parents didn't know was that it was Dominic who had been indirectly responsible for her decision to leave home and go to college, and ultimately to work in London. After that last traumatic meeting she had not been able to endure the thought of seeing him again, and so she had virtually run away. Quite needlessly, as it turned out, for Dominic himself had left Setondale that autumn to continue his medical studies in America.

Unable to stand the pressure of the old memories surging inside her, she paced the kitchen. She needed to get out, to breathe in the cool, calm air and gather her composure.

An old anorak from her college days was still hanging on its peg in the laundry-room, and she pulled it on with jerky, unco-ordinated movements.

Outside the sky had grown more leaden and menacing, the scent of snow stronger now. On the hills she could see a shepherd and his dog working the sheep, bringing them down to lower pastures. She started walking at a speed that set her hair bouncing on her shoulders, tension bracing her muscles, the cold air stinging her face. The path she took was a familiar one, climbing up towards the foothills, and gradually as she walked she felt her tension ease slightly. She passed the Vicarage, disturbing a dog that set up a clamorous barking. The house and its grounds had recently been sold, but she didn't pause to wonder about the new inhabitants of the sturdy Georgian building.

Dominic back! Her body shook with renewed tension and she expelled her breath on a pent-up sigh.

Her father had said that Dominic had had a soft spot for her. How little he knew. Savage by name and savage by nature, that was Dominic, and God, how she had suffered from that savagery!

With words that even now were engraved on her soul he had torn apart her childish fantasies and destroyed her innocence, holding up to her his contemptuous awareness of her adolescent feelings, giving her a distorted mirror-image of them that had scorched her with shame and anguish that still lived on in her soul.

It had all been her own fault, of course. She should have been content with simply worshipping him from a distance, and blissfully cherishing their long-standing friendship. Their parents had been friends, and from an early age she had attached herself to him even though he was eight years older. Dominic had lived with his parents in the house attached to the medical practice while he worked as a very junior doctor at the hospital in Alnwick. Her crush on him had developed the year she was sixteen. No doubt she would have been content with simply seeing him, and sighing over him, if it hadn't been for her school-friends.

For a reason she had never been able to define, during her last year at school she had been befriended by a crowd of girls led by the precocious daughter of their local MP. Helen Maguire was far more sophisticated and wordly than the other girls in the class, and she had sought out Christy as her best friend. How flattered and delighted she had been! Until then she hadn't had many friends. She was too quiet and shy to make friends easily, but she had glowed and relaxed in the flattering warmth of Helen's friendship, pushing aside her own doubts and natural reticence about the wisdom of joining in the giggled discussions on sex and boyfriends initiated by Helen. Naturally, since Helen was the one with the most experience, she was the one who did most of the talking, and although sometimes she had experienced a sense of revulsion when Helen described her sexual exploits, for the most part Christy had been caught too deep in the adolescent thrall of having such a wonderful friend to question too deeply Helen's values and morals.

Of course, it was as inevitable as night following day that Helen should worm out of her her feelings for Dominic, and that once having discovered them, she should exhort Christy not to be such a baby.

'If you want him, you ought to go out and get him,' she had informed Christy, giving her a sly sideways smile as she added softly, 'it's easy when you know how. Shall I tell you?'

The stitch in her side made Christy pause and lean momentarily against a large rock. A feeling of nausea gathered in the pit of her stomach as she tried to drag her thoughts away from the past. Remembering did no good . . . and no matter how often she went back she couldn't change the past; she couldn't wipe out or obliterate what had happened, no matter how much she might want to. She shuddered deeply as she drew in lungfuls of air, icy cold now that she had climbed above the valley bottom, stinging the inside of her chest. She welcomed the pain, because pain meant reality, and reality was *now*, eight years on from that awful summer.

She ought to have forgotten it long ago. Dominic

Savage's memory should have faded and been lost
beneath happier memories of other men, but it stood
between her and her fulfilment as a woman like some
sort of revenging spirit.

She smiled without mirth as she remembered
David's incredulous look of disbelief when she had
told him.

'You're still a virgin? But that's impossible! God,
Christy, a man only has to look at you! Those eyes . . .
that red hair . . . your body . . . *they* don't belong to
some chaste Victorian maiden.'

She hadn't been able to stop her mouth from
trembling, and he was sensitive and intuitive enough
to know that she wasn't lying. If only David hadn't
been married. How willingly she would have given
herself over to his sexual mastery. Physically she had
found him attractive, even while she knew she didn't
love him. She had wanted his lovemaking, his skill,
and his expertise, like some sort of sleeping princess
awaiting the awakening kiss of a prince, she thought
now, dourly. But she couldn't hurt Meryl, and so the
chasm of fear and self-loathing that Dominic had
blasted between her and her sexuality had remained
unbreached.

As she stood leaning against the stone, the first fine
flakes of snow began to fall. She knew that she ought
to go back, but she was unwilling to do so, unwilling to
face Dominic until she had made herself relive the full
horror of that awful night.

She wasn't going to blame Helen; the fault, the
desire had been hers. She was the one who had
listened with awed fascination to Helen's description
of how easy it was to seduce a man. The other girl's

voice had been edged with the contempt of an
intrinsically sexually cold female for the vulnerability
of the male, but then she had been too naïve to see it,
and so, round-eyed, and inwardly faintly shocked, she
had drunk in Helen's detailed instructions.

'But what if he doesn't . . . you know? What if he
doesn't make love to me?'

Helen had shrugged. 'You don't need to worry about
that. Once you've aroused him, he won't be able to
stop himself. None of them can.'

Alarm and excitement had twisted inside her;
excitement at the thought of Dominic making love to
her, and alarm at the thought of her own daring in
imagining that he might.

It had been quite easy to discover an evening when
Dominic would be at home alone. Every fortnight her
own parents and his met up to play bridge, and she
only had to wait until the venue for this fortnightly get-
together was her own home.

'Wear something sexy,' had been Helen's first
instruction. Easy enough to say, but there was nothing
in her wardrobe that remotely deserved such a
description.

In the end, feeling more uncomfortable and
embarrassed than sexy, she had taken off her bra, and
unfastened her cotton shirt to show the taut upper
swell of her breasts, before tugging it into her habitual
jeans.

A cardigan hid the evidence of her bra-less state
from her parents as she said her goodbyes, guilt and
desire mingling in almost equal quantities as she got
on her bike and sped down the drive.

It had been a hot summer, and the French windows

of the Savages' house stood open as she cycled down the drive and round to the back door.

Since their parents were close friends, it was not unusual for her to visit the house, but as she got off her bike she was filled with an awareness that she was trespassing, not just against the Savages' friendship but also against her parents' trust.

She would have turned back then if it hadn't been for the fact that she would have to face Helen in the morning, and so, quelling her feelings, she went round to the French windows and knocked briefly before walking in.

The sitting-room was empty; her heart thudding, she walked through into the hall, and then stood there transfixed as she saw Dominic coming towards her down the stairs, pulling on a white shirt.

His hair was damp, his skin tanned and firm against the powerful male muscles. Something seemed to expand and flower inside her, a deep pulsating excitement that brought a delicate flush of colour to her skin and deepened her eyes to dark jade.

'Christy, is everything all right?'

The sharpness in his voice brought her back to reality. 'Yes.'

'Then what are you doing here?' He was frowning at her as he buttoned his shirt, and because he had never before spoken to her in anything other than a teasingly indulgent voice, Christy could only stare at him. 'I asked you what you came here for.'

He was at the bottom of the stairs now, frowning at her, and even though she was tall she had to tilt back her head to look at him. She had taken off her cardigan as she stepped back from him, the dying rays

of the evening sun falling across the thin cotton of her
blouse, revealing the uncovered peaks of her breasts.

She heard Dominic catch his breath on what
sounded like an impatient sigh, and said hurriedly, 'I
. . . I came to see you . . .'

'Me?' He was frowning even more now. 'What
about?'

Panic flared inside her. This wasn't going the way it
should. By now he shouldn't be questioning her; he
should be looking at her . . . wanting her. It wasn't
going to be as easy as Helen had said. Confusion
flooded through her, and she turned puzzled, worried
eyes up to him, betraying more than she knew.

'I . . . I just wanted to talk to you,' she said lamely,
flushing a brilliant shade of red as he suddenly said
harshly, 'Christy, what's this all about? You aren't in
some . . . some kind of trouble, are you?'

Her eyes widened, and went brilliant with shock as
she absorbed his meaning. There was only one kind of
trouble he could mean, and she jerked back from him
indignantly.

'No . . . no, of course not! How could you think
anything like that . . .?' She was shocked and hurt that
he could think that she would give herself to anyone
other than him, barely taking in his curt, 'All too
easily, especially when you parade yourself around
dressed like that.' A flick of his hand indicated that he
was aware of her near-nudity, and she flushed again.
This wasn't the way he was supposed to react. Helen
had said . . .

She bit her lip and moved closer to him, her voice
shaking as she implored huskily, 'Dominic, please
don't be angry with me . . .' Tears weren't very far

away; she could feel them clogging up the back of her throat.

She heard him sigh, and then rapturously felt his arms go round her; she was being cradled against him, her head resting on his shoulder, the bare heat of his chest against her thinly covered breasts.

She quivered with nerves and excitement, aching to reach out and touch him, but scarcely able to even draw breath, never mind do anything else.

Helen was right, and it had worked! Her legs shook and threatened to give way beneath her. Her heart seemed to have lodged somewhere in her throat and was threatening to suffocate her. Could Dominic feel it beating? She could feel the steady, even thud of his. Instinctively she moved her hand to touch the place where she could feel that strong beat.

Her fingertips trembled against his skin and then, shockingly, almost frighteningly, her wrist was seized in an iron grip and she was forcefully pushed away from him.

Angry grey eyes glared down into the bemused jade of hers. 'Just what the hell do you think you're doing?'

The shock of his sudden withdrawal was too much for her to cope with. She was still lost in the rapturous dream of her own intense desire and love, and without comprehending his anger she burst out eagerly, 'Dominic, make love to me. Please ... I know you want to.'

For a moment it was as though they were frozen in time: she gazing pleadingly up at him, her mouth soft and trembling, her body, supple and eager for his touch; he, tense and angry, the grey eyes darkened almost to black, his mouth drawn in a tight hard line, his body tense as though he was too furious even to draw breath.

And then the spell was broken, and the reality of his anger crashed through her physical arousal as he breathed harshly, 'My God, I don't believe I'm hearing this. Is this why you came here dressed like . . . like . . . like a modern-day Lolita? To ask me to make love to you? And you're so damned blatant about it, as well!'

He saw the shock and pain on her face, and although she wasn't aware of it, his voice softened slightly. 'Christy, I can't make love to you . . . you know that.'

'Because you don't want me?' She made herself face him, and saw his face grow cold and shuttered.

'Among other things,' he agreed evenly, adding, 'it is customary for the woman to wait to be asked, you know. Who put you up to this? Come on, Christy, no lies. I know you; you'd never have thought of doing this for yourself.'

She had been too distraught and humiliated to keep back the truth, and he had kept on and on at her until she had told him everything. She had had to sit there answering his questions and seeing the look of contemptuous disgust darken his eyes, until he had moved away from her as though even to look at her had contaminated him.

'Well, now it's my turn to tell you something,' he had said at last, when she was finished. 'Contrary to what your friend informed you, it isn't that easy to make a man desire you.'

She had flushed with shame and pain then, but he hadn't let her look away, holding her chin with hard, hurting fingers as he said cruelly, 'Look at me, Christy. Go on . . . take a good look . . . your friend has told you what to look for. Do I *look* as though I want you physically?'

She had wanted to get up and run away then, but shock and pain had held her rigidly where she stood, shivering like a rabbit before a hawk, totally unable to do anything other than stare blindly back into his savagely dark eyes.

When she couldn't turn her eyes in the direction of his body, he taunted with soft menace, 'If you won't look at me, perhaps you'd like to touch me instead. Just so that you know I'm not lying to you . . .'

She had shuddered deeply then, knowing that he had just destroyed her childish illusions, exposing her as what she was, and how she had hated the image of herself that he had held up to her gaze! She had turned away from him then, struggling to subdue the sob of terror and anguish that rose up in her throat.

He hadn't let her go, though; there had been more for her to endure. A lecture about the physical dangers she was courting: about the health risk of promiscuity, about the danger of rape and worse, and a reminder of how much her parents loved and trusted her and how shocked they would be if they knew what she had done. Worse still, he hadn't let her ride home on her bike, but had sent her upstairs to the bathroom to wash her face and brush her hair, and once she had done that he had waited until she had buttoned herself into her concealing cardigan and then had driven her home.

There was only eight years between them, but he had been as stern and forbidding as any Victorian

parent, and when he had let her out of the car at the
end of her parents' drive she had known that she
would hate and loathe him for the rest of her life.

But not as much as she would hate herself, she
reflected bitterly as she emerged from the past and
came back to the present.

She had avoided Helen after that and had asked her
parents if, instead of going back to school, she could
attend college instead. They had agreed and found her
comfortable digs in Newcastle, where in addition to
her secretarial skills she had learned how to begin
living with herself again.

It was as though those hectic weeks when Helen had
been her friend had been some sort of sickness from
which she had emerged with a revulsion for all that
she had been and done. The very thought of meeting
Dominic in those early days had been enough to make
her feel physically ill, and if her parents thought it was
curious that she never mentioned him, they kept it to
themselves.

She sighed faintly. The snow was coming down
more heavily now. It was time for her to return home.
She glanced at her watch. Ten past three. Good, by the
time she got back Dominic should have left. She knew
she couldn't spend her entire life avoiding him, but
discovering that he was back had been such a shock.
She hadn't been ready for it. Now, having endured the
catharsis of making herself relive the past, she should
be stronger, more able to judge her teenage actions
with tolerance and compassion. But she couldn't. That
was the problem: she couldn't get over the feelings of
shame and self-disgust that Dominic had given her;
they still haunted and tainted her life like a disease

that, although dormant, still possessed the power to return.

She hated Dominic because of the picture he had drawn of her and made her face. She hated the fact that he had witnessed her shame and humiliation. She hated him because he made her hate herself.

Sighing, she pulled the hood of her anorak up against the snow and started for home.

CHAPTER TWO

SHE almost made it. She was just treading down the lane, head bowed against the snow, when she heard the car, and instinctively began to move out of the middle of the lane, but the snow had made it treacherous and she slipped and lost her balance, going down with a bump that robbed her of breath and jarred her body.

Christy was distantly aware of the car stopping and a door slamming, but it wasn't until he came and lifted her out of the snow that she realised who her rescuer was.

'Dominic!'

Her body froze in instant recognition and panic. Eight years hadn't changed him at all, except to make him seem more formidable. That aura of leashed power that had once so excited and intrigued her was still there; the black hair was still as thick and dark as ever, the grey eyes as alert. He even had the same deep tan, while she . . .

As he hauled her to her feet, she grimaced inwardly, bitterly aware of her soaked jeans and ancient anorak. Why on earth hadn't she taken the trouble to put on some make-up and do her hair? She could feel it tangling untidily round her head, and surely she might have had the sense to put on one of the stunning ski-suits she had bought for last winter's skiing holiday with David and his family.

Oh God, if she had to face Dominic, why on earth couldn't it have been with all the armour she had learned to adopt in the last eight years instead of this, looking much as she had done as a teenager, instead of the sophisticated woman she had learned to become?

'Christy, are you OK?'

Incredibly, he sounded concerned as he brushed the snow off her face and, even more astounding, he was smiling at her, a smile she recognised from before those traumatic days when she had tried to turn the casual affection of an adult male towards the young daughter of his parents' friends into something more personal. As she looked into his concerned eyes it was almost as though that dreadful summer had never been. She caught her breath at the shock of it. Surely he couldn't have forgotten . . .

No, of course he hadn't, but perhaps he judged it more politic to pretend he had. She stiffened and pushed him away, her brusque, 'I'm fine, no thanks to you,' causing his smile to change to a frown. 'Do you always drive about without any thought for the safety of others?' she demanded tartly. 'Hardly the sort of behaviour one would expect in a member of the medical profession.'

His smile had faded completely now, to be replaced by a sharp-eyed scrutiny of her pale, set face.

'I was driving slowly enough to be able to stop, and hardly anyone ever uses this lane,' he pointed out calmly.

Christy knew that she was over-reacting, but it was the only way she could hold at bay her shock at seeing him. She had thought she had managed to avoid him, and it struck her now that she would have much preferred to face him again in the familiarity of her own home rather than out here like this, when she was at such a disadvantage. Again she cursed her own folly in being stupid enough to try and avoid him. Far better if she had stayed at home and greeted him in one of the elegantly expensive outfits she wore for work—outfits that said quite unmistakably that she was an adult.

His eyes monitored her pale face and shaky limbs, his forehead furrowing in a deep frown.

'Are you sure you're all right?' He reached out to help her, and instinctively she recoiled.

'Get in the car,' he told her, still watching her. 'I'll run you home. It won't take me a minute, and as your family doctor, I . . .'

'You're not my doctor!'

The passionate denial was out before she could silence it, leaving them staring at one another, her, tense with shock, and Dominic narrow-eyed with an expression she could not interpret.

'Christy.'

His voice was clipped now, his dark eyebrows drawn together over those clear grey eyes, the dark head inclined towards her at an achingly familiar angle. 'Look, it's pointless us standing here arguing. It's a good half-mile to the house. Even if nothing's damaged, a fall like that can be quite a shock.'

Christy knew that it was pointless and childish trying to argue with him, especially with her nerve ends jumping like discordant wires and her heart beating so fast she could hardly draw breath. He was right, she was suffering from shock, but not because of her fall. With a brief shrug she moved towards his car—a brand new BMW, she noticed wryly, staring at the glossy paintwork. He moved towards her, his body brushing against hers as he opened the door. Instantly she stiffened and drew away.

'What's wrong?'

Did he really honestly need to ask?

'Nothing. I just don't like being touched, that's all.'

Too late she registered his expression. What she had said was quite true, and it was an excuse she had used so often that she was barely aware of the import of it any more, but as she brushed the snow off her anorak she was suddenly aware of Dominic studying her with a curiously fixed intensity.

Suddenly his mouth twisted, giving him a faintly satanic air, and she coloured hotly, knowing what he must be thinking, but knowing equally that there was no way she could refute his thoughts, or stop him from remembering a time when she had wanted far more than just his touch.

Feeling sick with reaction, she pulled back from the car. 'I don't want a lift, Dominic,' she told him huskily. 'I'd much rather walk,' and before he could stop her, she set off down the lane at a brisk pace, not daring to turn round in case she saw him following her.

It was an unnerving sensation, and one that turned her legs to rubber, but at last she made it to the garden gate, and it was only once she was inside that she heard the sound of Dominic's car engine firing, and realised that he must have watched her walk the whole way.

Well, of course, as a doctor, he could hardly have it said that he had neglected any of his responsibilities.

Her mouth curled bitterly as she limped towards the front door.

As she closed it behind her her father called out, 'Christy, is that you?' His study door opened and his eyebrows rose as he studied her wet clothes. 'You've just missed Dominic. What on earth happened to you? You look as though you had a fight with a snowdrift and came off worst!'

'You're almost right.'

She saw him frown. 'Are you OK?'

'Yes . . . I fell over in the lane. Fortunately nothing's damaged apart from my pride. How's Mum?'

'She's coming along very nicely, so Dominic says, but you'll be able to ask him for yourself tonight. He's coming for supper.' He looked guiltily at her. 'Your mother invited him. She worries about him, living all alone in the Vicarage. You know what a fusser she is.'

So it was Dominic who had bought the Vicarage. Christy's heart sank as she registered her father's words. She could hardly fabricate an excuse to absent herself tonight.

'You needn't worry about what to cook. Your mother said to tell you that the freezer's full. We miss Dominic's parents. The four of us used to have some good times together . . .'

Guiltily Christy chastised herself for her selfishness. Dominic's father had died four years ago, and then his mother had gone to live with her widowed sister in Berkshire. They had been her parents' closest friends, but until now all she had been conscious of was her own relief that their absence meant that there was no longer any reason for Dominic to return to Setondale. But he *had* returned . . .

'Is Mum awake? I thought I'd go up and see her.'

'Yes, do. She's complaining already that she's getting bored, but Dominic has told her that she has to stay in bed at least another week.'

Her mother was sitting propped up against her pillows when Christy walked into her parents' bedroom. Sarah Marsden was a striking-looking woman, with her daughter's green eyes and the high cheekbones of the Celtic Scots. She smiled warmly as she saw Christy, and patted the bed. 'There you are, darling. Come and sit down and talk to me. I'm bored out of my mind lying here, but Dominic insists.' She watched her daughter carefully as she added, 'You know, of course, that he's back?'

Sarah Marsden had far more intuition than her husband, and she was well aware of her daughter's reluctance to talk about anything or anyone connected with Dominic Savage. She knew about her adolescent crush on him, of course; it had been glaringly obvious, but Dominic had been at pains to treat her gently. She had never fathomed out what it was that had led to Christy's abhorrence of the very mention of his name, and she knew her daughter far to well to pry. Instead she said calmly, 'I invited Dominic to come round for supper. A man living on his own never eats properly.'

'Nonsense, Mum,' Christy interrupted crisply, 'there's no reason why on earth a man shouldn't be able to take care of himself in much the same way as a woman has to.'

'Oh, I wasn't suggesting thát Dominic wasn't *capable* of looking after himself, Christy,' her mother corrected gently. 'I'm sure he can. But as a very busy doctor, I'm also sure that he doesn't have the time to do more than grab the odd snack. There's a ragout in the freezer; I thought you might give him that. It always used to be his favourite . . .'

'Stop worrying about Dominic Savage and try and get some rest,' Christy instructed her. Really, her mother was impossible at times! Here she was recuperating from major heart surgery and all she could think about was Dominic Savage's stomach.

It wasn't because she wanted to impress Dominic that she took particular pains with her appearance that night, Christy told herself, donning an elegantly sophisticated jersey dress that David had urged her to buy from a shop in South Molton Street.

The camel-coloured jersey, so dull on anyone else, on her was the perfect foil for her copper hair, the knitted material designed to cling lovingly to every inch of her body. Despite the fact that it covered her from throat to knees, it was undoubtedly a dress designed for women with men in mind. Which no doubt was why David had chosen it in the first place, she thought wryly, remembering her own doubts the day she had tried it on. That had been before David had told her how he felt about her. Her mouth compressed slightly as she busied herself blow-drying her unruly curls into sleek copper order.

Now her make-up: just the merest hint of green eyeshadow, and then mascara to darken the blonde tips of her eyelashes. Blusher to emphasise her cheekbones, and then the merest slick of lip gloss. She stood up and slipped on her high heels, smiling rather grimly at her reflection.

Yes . . . This was the woman she now was, not the child she had once been. No one looking at her now

could doubt her maturity. As she walked away from
the mirror she didn't see the glimmer of vulnerability
that darkened her eyes, nor the soft quiver of her
mouth.

Her father's eyebrows lifted slightly as she walked
into the kitchen, but he was familiar enough with her
London clothes and the sophistication that went with
it not to make any comment. She found the ragout in
the freezer and started the preparations for supper.
She couldn't very well avoid eating with her father and
Dominic, but once the meal was over she intended to
excuse herself on the pretext that she was tired. After
all, she thought cynically, Dominic could hardly want
her company.

A pain, as though someone had twisted a knife in
her heart, tore through her as she remembered the
open warmth of his smile, for all the world as though
he *had* actually been glad to see her. No doubt there
were times when a doctor needed to conceal his true
feelings, and he had obviously more than mastered
that art.

Her mother wasn't allowed any heavy meals, so just
before Dominic was due, Christy took her up a light
snack.

'Oh, very nice; I do like that, Christy,' Mrs Marsden
approved, as she studied her daughter's dress. Despite
the fact that she lived a rural existence, Sarah
Marsden had retained a vivid interest in fashion and
was able to comment knowledgeably on her daughter's outfit.

'David chose it,' Christy told her, failing to notice
the look of concern darkening her mother's eyes. 'I
wasn't sure if it was really me, but you know what he's

like. He overruled all my objections.'

'Yes, he can be a very forceful man. And a very magnetic one as well ...' She paused, and Christy looked across at her.

'You've always seemed so happy in your job, Christy. Your father and I were a bit surprised to hear that you'd given it up. I hope it wasn't anything to do with this silly heart of mine.'

'It wasn't,' Christy assured her truthfully. 'As I told Dad this morning, David has been offered some work in Hollywood, and since there's every chance that he might stay on over there, naturally I couldn't go on working for him.'

'But he could have taken you with him.'

Christy could sense the direction of her mother's thoughts. 'Yes, I suppose he could,' she agreed airily. 'But he didn't, and quite fortunately, as it turns out that that means I'm free to come home and spend some time with you. Unless, of course, you're trying to tell me that my help isn't wanted ...'

'Christy, darling, this is your home. We're both delighted to have you back. Umm ... that sounds like Dominic's car. You'd better go down and let him in. Your father will never hear him. He's getting dreadfully deaf, you know.'

Reluctantly Christy headed for the door. As her mother had predicted, the sound of the doorbell had not brought her father out of his study, so she made her way down to the hall, shivering in the blast of cold air that swirled in as she opened the front door.

Dominic had changed out of the suit he had been wearing earlier and was now dressed casually in navy pants and a matching jacquard sweater. His eyebrows rose as he saw her, and for a moment something almost like pain seemed to flicker in his eyes.

'I'll just tell my father that you're here,' Christy told him formally, stepping away from him. 'Supper shouldn't be long.'

Her father, roused from his study, apologised to Dominic for not hearing the bell.

'I persuaded Christy that we'd be better off eating in the kitchen. Our dining-room faces north and it's freezing in there at this time of the year. Come on in, and sit down.'

Christy gnawed anxiously at her bottom lip as she followed them. The very last thing she had wanted was to have Dominic sharing the warm intimacy of the kitchen with them, watching her while she worked . . . it made no difference that there had once been a time when her parents' kitchen had been as familiar to him as his own, and she resented his easy assumption that all was as it had once been. Surely he must be aware how hard it was for her to have to face him like this, but he was behaving as though nothing had happened, as though he had never humiliated and hurt her in a way that was branded into her heart for all time.

While she busied herself putting the finishing touches to their supper, Christy could hear her father and Dominic chatting, and yet she was also conscious, every time she happened to glance at him, that Dominic was also watching her. *Watching* her, she thought shakily, not just simply looking at her. What was he watching her for? Did he think she was going to fling herself at him and beg him to make love to her? Did he think that she was still suffering from that dreadful teenage crush?

'Ragout. My favourite.' Dominic smiled at her as she served out the meal, but she refused to smile back.

'Your mother tells me that you've given up your job in London.'

'The man I worked for is going out to Hollywood.' Although it was impossible to refuse to answer Dominic's questions with her father smiling benignly at them, she kept her answers as curt and clipped as possible, and after several attempts at conversation with her, all of which she blocked, she saw his mouth compress into a hard line and a steely glint darken his eyes.

The phone rang in the hall, and her father got up to answer it. While he was gone Dominic took advantage of his absence to say curtly, 'What's wrong, Christy?'

That he should actually need to ask her robbed her of the breath with which to answer him, and by the time she had recovered her wits, her father was back in the kitchen.

For the rest of the meal Dominic directed his conversation almost exclusively towards her father. Eight years ago she would have felt hurt and left out and would have made a childish attempt to break into their discussions, but now she was glad to be left alone.

After supper, her father's suggestion that he and Dominic play a game of chess left Christy free to clear up the kitchen and then go upstairs to check on her mother.

'You needn't sit up here with me, dear,' Sarah Marsden told her. 'I'm perfectly all right. In fact, I was just thinking I'd like to go to sleep. Why don't you go back downstairs and join your father and Dominic?'

'They're playing chess.'

Her mother laughed. 'Oh dear, I remember how you always used to resent that. Dominic tried to teach you to play several times, didn't he?'

Memories she didn't want to acknowledge surged over her; an image of her petulant sixteen-year-old face pouting protestingly as she tried to divert Dominic's attention from his game to herself. That had been in the days before she had realised the true nature of the strange restlessness that seemed to possess her.

'You were always far too restless to concentrate,' her mother added fondly. 'I remember one Sunday afternoon, you picked up the board and threw all the pieces on to the floor.'

'The year I took my O-levels. Dominic threatened to wallop me for it.'

'Yes, I remember.' Her mother laughed, and Christy wondered if she also remembered how that miserable afternoon had ended. *She* certainly did.

For weeks she had been troubled by a vague but persistent feeling of restlessness; she wanted to be with Dominic, but when she was, she wasn't satisfied with their old comfortable friendship. Too young and inexperienced to be able to analyse her own feelings, she had taken refuge in fits of sulks alternated with bursts of temper. Dominic's threat to put her over his knee and administer the punishment he thought she deserved had acted like a shock of cold water on her newly emerging feminine feelings, and she had retreated from him to the sanctuary of her bedroom, in floods of tears.

The next day he had been waiting for her when she came out of school. He had driven her half-way home and had then stopped the car on a secluded piece of road.

'I'm sorry about last night, infant,' he had said softly. 'I forget sometimes that you're not a little girl any more.'

She had burst into tears again, but this time there had been nowhere to run and she had sobbed out her misery and confusion against the hard warmth of his shoulder, even in her anguish conscious of the pleasure of his body close to her own and his arms wrapped round her.

He had kissed her briefly on the forehead as he released her, offering his handkerchief so that she could dry her eyes. That had been the day she knew she had fallen in love with him.

'Come back, Christy . . .'

Her mother's teasing voice jolted her back to the present and reality, and although she listened to her chatter as she smoothed her pillows and checked that she had everything she needed, Christy was wondering what her mother would say if she told her that now she *could* play chess. Meryl had taught her. Meryl, whose patience made her an admirable teacher; Meryl, whose patience allowed her to turn a blind eye to a husband to whom a continuous string of brief sexual affairs seemed to be as necessary as the air he breathed. And yet without Meryl, David would be very unhappy. She was his wife, and in his way he loved her. He also loved their children. Sighing faintly, Christy walked towards the door. Adult relationships were very complex things. As a teenager she had daydreamed about the perfect life she would have with Dominic if he loved her; she had imagined that love alone was enough, that nothing else mattered, but different people had different needs.

She herself was too old-fashioned in her moral outlook to involve herself in an affair with a married man, especially a married man whose wife she knew and liked.

No matter how awkward and unsettling it was discovering that Dominic had come back to Seton-dale, she knew that she had made the right decision in refusing to accompany David to Hollywood. Already, the effect of his sexual magnetism was beginning to fade now that he was no longer there to generate it. Maybe even the desire she had felt clawing so sharply within her had really been the desire of an inexperienced woman for experience rather than a particular desire for David himself.

Ever since the humiliation of her rejection by Dominic, Christy had kept the sexual side of her nature firmly under control. She was not and never had been the sort of woman to whom sex could be sufficient in itself, but there were times, increasingly so these days, when she saw lovers embracing, couples together, when she was pierced by an intense need, coupled with sadness for all that she had lost in not having a lover of her own.

And that was Dominic's fault; his strictures, his contempt had made it impossible for her to be open and honest in her dealings with his sex; she was quite frankly terrified of misinterpreting a man's feelings and suffering once again the savage rejection which still haunted her.

She went downstairs and started to make a tray of coffee for her father and Dominic. It was gone ten o'clock and, as Dominic no doubt remembered, her parents preferred early nights.

When she took the tray in it was obvious that Dominic was winning the game.

'He's got me completely tied up,' her father commented with a mock grimace as she handed him his coffee.

'Mmm.' She studied the chess board knowledgeably. 'Another two moves and you won't be able to avoid checkmate.'

Her father's eyebrows rose, but he looked pleased. 'Well, well, so you *have* managed to learn something while you've been in London!' Turning to Dominic, he asked teasingly, 'Do you remember how often you tried to teach her?'

'There are teachers and teachers,' Christy responded acidly, watching the way Dominic frowned as he looked up at her. The humour she had seen warming his eyes earlier was gone now, and they were a hard, flat grey.

'And pupils and pupils,' he taunted back, while her father looked from one set face to the other as though suddenly conscious of the fast-flowing undercurrents racing between them.

Christy was glad that the phone rang, cutting through the thick silence. Her father went to answer it, and she started to follow him until Dominic's smooth voice stopped her.

'You've changed, Christy. And I don't suppose for one moment that chess is the only thing you've been taught!'

She swung round, her eyes glittering with the temper he had always been so easily able to arouse inside her, but before she could say anything, her father came back into the room, frowning slightly.

'The call's for you, Christy. It's David.'

'My ex-boss. I suppose he's lost an all-important piece of filing.' She knew she was flushing and that moreover, Dominic was aware of it, but David ringing her when she had thought she had made it quite clear to him that there was no point in him pursuing her had caught her off guard.

She hurried to the phone, curling the flex round her fingers in nervous agitation as she spoke into the receiver.

'Christy, my love, you can't know how much I've missed hearing your voice. I miss you, Christy. Come back.'

She gritted her teeth together. She had always known that David was persistent when there was something that he wanted, but she thought she had made it clear there could be nothing between them.

'I can't come back, David,' she responded coolly. 'My mother is ill and she needs me.'

'*I* need you. God, how I need you! Come back, Christy . . .'

Her body had started to tremble. This was too much to cope with coming on top of her clash with Dominic.

'I can't, David.' She took a deep breath. 'And I wouldn't even if I could. I've already told you that. You're a married man. You know how much I like Meryl.'

'Oh, for God's sake!' she heard him swear sharply. 'Listen, Christy . . .'

Suddenly she panicked. 'No . . . no . . . I don't want to hear any more.' She held the receiver away from her, but before she could slam it down she heard him saying furiously, 'I'm not letting you go as easily as that. I want you . . . and I can make you want me . . .'

Even with the receiver held away from her, the words were plainly audible. She slammed it down, literally shaking with reaction.

'And that's your boss, is it?'

The shock of Dominic's hard voice coming from behind her made her whirl round to stare at him.

Correctly reading her expression, he added evenly, 'I just came in to say goodnight, on your father's instructions. I didn't mean to eavesdrop. Do you love him, Christy . . . is that why you've come running home?'

'He's a married man.' She cried out the words desperately, hating him for seeing her like this when she was so weak and vulnerable.

'I see . . .'

Surely that wasn't compassion she could see in his eyes. She shook her head disbelievingly and heard him say, 'If there's anything I can do to help . . .'

Eight years ago she had needed his help, but he had rejected her, and suddenly she wanted to throw that in his face, and to tell him that it was his fault she was the person she was now; that it was his fault that she was a twenty-four-year-old virgin with ridiculously unrealistic ideals of love and marriage, but common sense told her that the blame wasn't all his, so instead she stormed past him, saying bitterly, 'Stop trying to big-brother me, Dominic; I don't need your help, either as a doctor or as a man.'

His face closed up immediately, and she was conscious of an unfamiliar hardness about it, an expression that warned her that he would be a dangerous man to push too hard.

'I'll say goodnight, then.' He paused in the act of stepping past her to the front door and said quietly, 'Just tell me one thing. Was he . . .' he gestured to the phone, 'the one who taught you to play chess?'

Briefly she frowned. 'No . . . no . . . he wasn't . . .'

What an odd thing to ask her. She was just about to ask him the reason for his question, but he opened the door and stepped through it before she could do so.

'Dominic gone, then?' her father asked, coming into the hall a moment later. 'He's a nice lad. Clever, too.'

Christy's eyebrows rose as she went into his study to collect the coffee cups. 'If he's so clever then what's he doing coming to work here as a mere GP? I thought he would have been better off staying in America?'

'Financially, maybe,' her father agreed, his expression slightly reproving. 'But the Savage men have been general practitioners here for three generations, and Dominic has a tremendous sense of duty. He alway did have; don't you remember how protective he always used to be of you? We never needed to worry about you when you were in Dominic's care.'

'I would have thought he had more ambition than to want to spend all his life in Setondale.'

'Oh, he's got ambition all right. He was telling me tonight about his hopes and plans. He wants to try to raise enough money locally to buy and equip a local surgery that's capable of carrying out most of the more common operations. He's seen it done in the States and is convinced it can be copied here, and I think he'll do it, too. There's going to be quite a lot of work involved in raising the initial finance, of course, but I've promised to give him what help I can—oh, and I told him that you'd probably be prepared to take on the secretarial side of things for him. It's a very worthwhile cause, and I'm sure he'll be able to get a lot of local support. After all, it's going on for forty miles to the nearest hospital, and the sort of clinic-cum-operating theatre Dominic plans for Setondale could only benefit everyone.'

Her father's enthusiasm for Dominic's plans made it impossible for Christy to tell him that there was no way she was going to be involved in anything that brought her into closer contact with Dominic. She tried to comfort herself with the conviction that she was the very last person Dominic would want to assist him, but she couldn't help remembering that since his unexpected return he had behaved as though that final annihilating scene between them had simply never taken place. Maybe *he* could do that, but she couldn't. Every time she looked at him she remembered her humiliation.

Thoroughly infuriated and exasperated by her father's lack of intuition in realising that she wanted nothing whatsoever to do with Dominic, she carried the coffee tray into the kitchen.

CHAPTER THREE

FOUR days passed without Christy seeing anything of Dominic. She told herself that she was glad, and concentrated on settling into a proper routine. By the end of the week she was finding that she had time to spare, and because she was used to being busy, it weighed heavily upon her hands. So heavily, in fact, that her father's announcement that a meeting was going to be held to discuss the setting-up of a committee to organise fund-raising for Dominic's clinic-cum-operating theatre came as a welcome relief.

'I've volunteered you to take notes and keep the minutes,' he warned her. 'Dominic was a bit dubious about whether you'd want to be so closely involved.'

Meaning that *he* didn't want her closely involved? She felt a totally unexpected pain shaft through her, which she suppressed instantly, instead concentrating on fanning her anger.

'Was he? Well, you can tell Dominic from me that I do want to do it. It will stop my secretarial skills from getting too rusty.'

'You'll be able to tell him for yourself,' her father chuckled. 'He's coming round for supper tonight, so that we can make a few preliminary plans.'

The sudden lurch of her heart was so intensely reminiscent of her reaction to the mention of his name at seventeen that it drove all the colour from her face.

What was the matter with her? She wasn't that susceptible, adolescent, any more. She felt nothing for Dominic Savage, unless it was dislike.

'Who else will be at the meeting?' she asked her father, trying to distract herself.

'Oh, John Howard, from the bank. He's bringing a client of his who's just moved into the area. A self-made man who's just retired and who he thinks might be interested in making a donation. I think I've managed to persuade Lady Anthony to join us. She suffers quite badly from arthritis now, and isn't as involved in local affairs as she was once, but I think she'll consider this is something worth being involved with. She's always had a soft spot for Dominic.'

'Yes. Ever since he presented her with the chocolates he won at the summer fête!'

Her father gave her an indulgent smile. 'Yes, you'd plagued the life out of him to give those chocolates to you.'

'And he said they weren't good for me.'

That had been the summer she was eleven, and Dominic had been, what? Nineteen and at medical school. She had adored him then, and he had put up with her adoration in much the same way as he might have tolerated the friskiness of an untrained puppy.

'Lady Anthony has a relative staying with her at the moment. I haven't met her, but I have heard that she's a very attractive young woman. You'll probably find you have quite a lot in common with her. She's been living in London, but when her marriage broke up she came to stay with her godmother. The Vicar will be there of course—oh, and Major Barnes.'

When Christy's eyebrows rose, her father grinned.

'Yes, I know. He and Lady Anthony will argue like mad. They always do, and secretly, I'm sure both of them enjoy it. He's an indefatigable organiser, though. We're all meeting at Dominic's house—you know he's bought the Vicarage.' He glanced apologetically at her. 'I'm afraid I've volunteered you to take charge of the refreshments. Your mother . . .'

Christy sighed, not needing him to finish the sentence. Yes, had she been well enough, her mother would have been the first to offer her services. Like the Major, her mother was also an indefatigable organiser, and many was the hot summer afternoon when Christy had been detailed to assist with a mammoth cake-baking session for some local bring-and-buy sale or summer fête.

It must be her nostalgia for those long-ago times that made her refrain from objecting to her father's casual disposal of her time, she decided the next morning as she surveyed the cooling sponges on their wire trays.

The inhabitants of Setondale were old-fashioned about some things; bought cakes were one of them. No self-respecting Setondale housewife would ever serve her visitors with something she had not prepared with her own hands.

Well, at least she didn't appear to have lost her touch with a sponge, Christy thought approvingly as she tested the golden-brown confectionery. In addition to the sponges, there were biscuits, made to her mother's special recipe, and later on she would make sandwiches and carefully cover them to stop them curling at the edges. She would have to borrow her father's car to run them over to Dominic's house, but

since her father was out playing golf with one of his
cronies he was hardly likely to object.

As she drove over to the Vicarage later in the day
Christy wondered curiously why Dominic had bought
it. Surely a smaller house in the centre of Setondale
itself would have suited him more? The very reason
the Church had sold off the Vicarage was its size, and
the cost of maintaining and heating it. As far as she
remembered, it had at least seven bedrooms, and then
there were the attics.

The wrought-iron gates were permanently open;
indeed, they had stood open for so long that she
doubted they could ever be closed. Weeds and
brambles had grown in between the spars, and the
bright winter sunshine highlighted their neglected
state.

The drive to the house too was overgrown, and the
trees, which would look lovely in the spring, now
looked gaunt and dreary without their leaves. Even so,
the Georgian façade of the house was undeniably
elegant, and the gardens, encircled as they were by a
high brick wall, would be a haven of privacy once they
had been brought under control. But who was going to
do that? Not Dominic, surely? He would be far too
busy.

As she parked her father's car and climbed out it
struck her that the Vicarage was very much a family
house. Did that mean that Dominic had plans to
marry? Her mind shied away from the thought.

As she approached the house the front door opened
and Dominic came out. Dressed casually in ancient
jeans and a plaid shirt, with the sleeves rolled up to his
elbows, he could almost once again have been the boy

she had adored as a child, and then he moved and the bright sunlight caught the harsh planes of his face, and the illusion of the boy was gone and she was faced with the reality of the man.

'I've just brought the eats for tonight.'

'I didn't think you'd come round just for the pleasure of my company.' The dry remark made her stop and look at him. 'Oh, come on, Christy, I'm not blind,' he said. 'You've made it more than obvious how you feel about me.'

She tensed then, unable to stop herself, alarm feathering over her skin as he came towards her. What did he mean? Her heart was pounding frantically, her throat dry. Surely she hadn't . . .

'It's obvious that you dislike me,' he continued curtly, and she felt her body sag with relief. He thought she disliked him. But he was right, she did . . . of course she did . . . Disliked and despised him . . . just as he had once despised her. 'However, we live in such a small community that we can't avoid one another,' he continued.

She managed to gather enough composure to say hardily, 'There's a difference between not avoiding one another and me falling over you almost every time I walk in the front door.'

She saw the way the planes of his face altered, his muscles tensing under the self-control he was using.

'Your parents happen to be old friends, and I'm damned if I'm going to give that friendship up just to suit you.'

She watched his jaw clench as he grated the words out at her, and then suddenly he turned to her, his body relaxing slightly as he appealed, 'Look, Christy,

what is it? We used to be such good friends ... I
accept that times, and people, change, but I can't
understand this ... this antipathy you have towards
me.'

He couldn't *understand*? A wave of anger shook her.
He had destroyed her world and now it seemed he
couldn't even remember doing it.

'No, I'm sure you can't,' she agreed tautly. 'But the
days are long gone when I grovelled at your feet,
Dominic, glad of every little scrap of attention you
threw my way. Let's just say that I've grown up, shall
we, and leave it at that.'

As she walked away from him and back to the car
she could hardly believe that he had actually forgotten
what had happened. Bitterness mingled with her
anger. How could she ever have been so stupid as to
invest him with all the virtues of some chivalrous
knight? The Dominic she had loved had never really
existed; he had simply been a figment of her
imagination. It was ridiculous that she should feel so
... so betrayed that he couldn't remember what he
had done to her, but she did.

This time as she walked towards the house carrying
her boxes of food he made no attempt to speak to her,
simply preceding her into the old-fashioned kitchen
and showing her where she could put everything.

'You don't have to do this, you know,' he told her
when she had finished. 'I can get someone else to act
as committee secretary.'

'Yes, I'm sure you can, but as I told my father, it will
stop my secretarial skills from getting rusty. Don't
flatter yourself that the fact that I have to come into
contact with you affects my decisions on how I live my

life, Dominic. It's simply that you're someone I'd rather not see unless I have to.'

'So I see. Well, if that's the case, you have my promise that I won't encroach on our old friendship. I had hoped . . .' He shrugged and turned away from her, but not before she had seen the bitterness twisting his mouth.

Dominic, bitter? But why? And what had he meant about him not encroaching on their old friendship? Surely *he* was the one who didn't want *her* encroaching on it, just as he had made plain to her eight years ago?

Feeling thoroughly confused, Christy headed back to her father's car. It was almost as though Dominic was trying to pretend that he wanted to be friends with her. But why? She wondered whether he was ashamed of the way he had treated her. But if that was the case, why didn't he say so; why pretend that he couldn't even remember that it had happened? It was like a jigsaw puzzle with all the vital pieces missing. For eight years she had harboured her resentment and dislike of him, and on hearing that he was back in Setondale she had expected that he would want as little contact with her as she did with him, and yet today he had implied that he wanted to resurrect their friendship.

At seven o'clock that evening, having made sure that her mother had everything she wanted, Christy and her father set out for the Vicarage. The temperature had dropped again, but the full moon had brought a clear sky with no threat of snow.

'We will have some yet, though,' her father predicted as he drove down the lane.

Little pockets from the previous week's snowfall

still lingered in hollows and by the roadside, and Christy was glad she wasn't driving when she felt the car start to slide once or twice.

They were the first to arrive, and Christy went straight to the kitchen, leaving her father and Dominic to talk. The anger against Dominic which had sustained her for so long seemed to have dissipated, leaving her feeling on edge and unsure of herself. She felt uncomfortable being near him, constantly tense and apprehensive, although why she was no longer sure. It was obvious to her now that he wasn't going to resurrect the past, as she had dreaded him doing, so why did she suffer from this inability to relax, even to breathe properly, when he was around?

During her years in London she had learned to deal with many difficult and fraught situations. Not even when she had had to refuse David had she experienced this degree of nervous constraint. It was almost as though Dominic possessed some special sort of power over her that made her intensely and uncomfortably aware of him. Even now, with the thickness of two walls separating them, she was acutely conscious of his presence. She didn't even need to look at him when he spoke to visualise his expressions. She could have drawn his every feature perfectly from memory. She shivered suddenly, and told herself it was the old stone house that made her feel so cold.

'Coffee ready?' her father called cheerfully, coming into the kitchen. 'The others seem to have arrived together.'

'It will only be a minute; I'll bring it through into the library.'

As she already knew, the Vicarage had four main

downstairs rooms in addition to the large and old-fashioned kitchen. There was a huge drawing-room, which the Vicar had never used; a dining-room, a comfortable sitting-room, and then the library. The library had always been her favourite room, with its smell of leather book bindings and dusty parchments. It overlooked the rear grounds of the house, and three of the walls were lined from floor to ceiling with mahogany bookcases. The Vicarage and the living that went with it had originally been in the gift of the Anthony family, and the house had been built for a younger son who had joined the clergy, hence its generous proportions.

Carrying the tray of coffee, Christy nudged open the door with her foot. Several pairs of eyes studied her entrance, but only two of them drew her attention. The first belonged to Dominic, and she felt the colour bloom under her skin as she realised how instinctively she had looked for him. There was a curious expression in the grey eyes, and if she hadn't known better she might have thought it was pleasure.

Angrily she dragged her glance away from Dominic's, and found that she was being stared at rather hostilely by a pair of cold blue eyes set in a sculptured but rather hard face which she deduced belonged to Lady Anthony's god-daughter.

'Ah, there you are, my dear.' Her father got up to relieve her of the tray, but Dominic beat him to it, which was rather strange as he had been seated furthest away from her.

'I think you know everyone, don't you, with the exception of Amanda, and Mr Bryant?'

Amanda Hayes' cold blue eyes acknowledged the

introduction without making any attempt to make Christy feel welcome. Wondering what on earth she had done to merit the other woman's patent hostility, Christy turned her attention to the older man seated with John Howard, their bank manager.

Somewhere in his fifties, he had the lean, predatory look of a man who challenged life head on, and Christy could easily visualise him in the role of a successful businessman.

Having made sure that everyone had something to eat and drink, she looked for somewhere to sit, and to her disquiet found that the only empty chair was one next to Dominic. Since he was obviously chairing the meeting she supposed it made good sense that she should sit next to him, but she saw from the narrow-eyed look that Amanda gave her that the other woman was equally displeased with the seating arrangements.

So that was the reason for her hostility, Christy thought as she sat down. Amanda couldn't know Dominic very well if she thought that *she* was any threat to her.

The next two hours passed so quickly that Christy had no time for any private mental meanderings. Her fingers flew over the notepad as she faithfully recorded the details of the meeting. Their first task, Dominic informed them, was to find somewhere suitable to convert into a clinic.

'I believe I've found the ideal place—a pair of Victorian semis that are up for sale in Setondale itself.'

There then followed a spirited discussion on the rival merits of buying a building and converting it, or having something purpose-built.

'Purpose-built is ideal, of course,' Dominic agreed.

'But because of the historic and architectural nature of Setondale, I'm afraid we might have problems with the planning and environmental people if we wanted to start right from scratch.'

'Well, I think the best thing for us to do is to go along and look at these semis,' Peter Bryant announced. He got out his diary and consulted it. 'I can manage tomorrow afternoon. After that I'm not free for two weeks.'

There were murmurs of assent from the other members of the committee, which concluded with the Major saying briskly, 'Right, that's settled, then; tomorrow afternoon it is. I'll liaise with the estate agents, and organise cars to make sure everyone can get there. I take it everyone wants to see the place.'

Everyone, it seemed, did, except Christy's father, who announced that since Christy could go in his stead, and since her presence was more necessary than his, she should go and he would stay at home with his wife.

'That's settled, then. I'll pick you up on the way, Christy,' suggested Dominic.

Instantly Amanda pouted, her hard eyes flashing warning signs at Christy. 'Dominic, I was going to ask if you would drive my godmother and me there . . . I'm afraid I'm rather useless behind the wheel of a car.'

'I . . .'

'Please don't worry about me, Dominic,' Christy intervened. 'I'm quite happy to drive myself. In fact, I'd prefer it,' she added, giving him a tight little smile. 'I don't like to be away from Mother for too long . . .'

Both of them knew that she was lying, but apart from the ominous tightening of his mouth, Dominic made no comment.

What had he expected? Christy asked herself in guilty defiance. That she would fling herself at his feet, with her old childish gratitude for his attention?

'Well, now that we've got that out of the way I suggest we move on to ways and means of raising the finance for this project.'

That was the Major, and as her pencil flew over her notebook again, Christy concentrated on recording the committee's suggestions on how the money might best be raised.

'As an incentive, my client, Peter Bryant, here, is prepared to donate twice the amount you can raise from the general public towards this new health centre,' John Howard added, when the others had finished speaking.

It was a very generous offer, and Christy wasn't the only person to look across at the entrepreneur when the bank manager had made his announcement.

'That's extremely generous of you,' said Dominic warmly.

'That remains to be seen, doctor—my generosity depends on how much you can raise by your own endeavours—God helps those who help themselves, eh?'

Christy guessed from the expression on the Vicar's face that he wasn't wholly at ease with the quotation, but whatever the man's motives, there was no getting away from the fact that his offer was a generous one.

Suspecting that the meeting was about to be concluded, Christy was just on the point of getting up to collect the coffee cups when Lady Anthony surprised her by saying, 'I have a suggestion to

make—actually it's my god-daughter's.' She smiled
fondly at her companion. 'She has reminded me that
we have an excellent and very large ballroom at the
Manor, and she has suggested that we hold a
Valentine's Night Ball there.'

'That's an excellent idea,' John Howard commented enthusiastically, before anyone else could
intervene. 'I know several customers of the bank who
would want to attend, especially if we could organise
some sort of supper.'

'You'll need a band, of course.' That was Amanda
herself speaking, her cold eyes sweeping dismissingly
around the table until they met Christy's as she added,
'And I expect there are plenty of women in and around
Setondale who could organise the food.'

In view of everyone else's enthusiasm, not even the
Major could decry the project, and Christy was
privately amused to see his desire to outmanoeuvre his
old rival, Lady Anthony, warring with his duties as
Chairman of the Finance Committee.

At last, grudgingly, he agreed that the idea was a
good one, and added that he thought he knew where
he could find their musicians.

'They'll be good ones, I hope,' Amanda chipped in.
'I mean, this won't be a dreary local hop. I intend to
ask some of my London friends to come down.'

Privately Christy suspected that if Amanda could
have excluded everyone bar her London friends and,
of course, Dominic, she would have been more than
pleased to do so, but it wasn't her job to make any
comments, only to take the minutes, which made it all
the more surprising when Dominic turned to her to
ask her, 'What do you think of the idea, Christy? Do

you think it will be well subscribed?'

She hesitated for a moment before replying, conscious that they were being watched. It was one thing for her to harbour her own resentment and dislike of Dominic; it was quite another to make everyone else aware of her feelings.

'Yes, yes, I think it will,' she answered after some deliberation. 'There are enough comfortably off people living locally for the tickets to sell very well.' She paused for a moment and added slowly, 'It's nothing to do with me . . . and it's only an idea, but since it is to be for Valentine's Night, how about making it a masked ball—not fancy dress as such, just masked.'

Out of the corner of her eye she saw the vindictive look in Amanda's eyes and sighed. She would have done better to say nothing, but the idea had just occurred to her and she had thought it a good one.

To her surprise, someone else did as well. After harrumping and frowning for several seconds, to not just her astonishment but everyone else's too, the Major cleared his throat and announced, 'Damn fine idea. Went to several when I was out in India. Damn fine affairs. Very romantic . . . Just the ticket for . . . er . . . Valentine's Night.'

The idea of the Major finding anything romantic was quite obviously as startling to the others as it was to her, and it was almost a full minute before anyone could speak. However, eventually Lady Anthony said firmly, 'I agree. I attended several such balls in my youth and they were all great fun.'

'Right, so a masked ball it will be.' Dominic turned to Christy, smiling at her with such warmth and

sincerity that she literally felt herself holding her
breath. She remembered that smile from long ago, and
the effect it had had on her—once, but not now, she
reminded herself, hardening her heart.

'I suppose we'd better select a sub-committee to
organise the details. I nominate Christy as ... er ...
organiser, and chief liaison person. I also vote that we
appoint Lady Anthony as Chairwoman.'

A regal inclination of her head confirmed that Her
Ladyship was pleased to accept such an office,
although Christy knew from observing her mother's
experience that she would be the one who was called
upon to do all the running around. Not that she
minded, she needed something to occupy those hours
when she was not taking care of her mother, and
organising the ball wasn't likely to bring her into any
contact with Dominic.

The Major was appointed to take care of the
financial side of things, and Christy wondered if she
was the only one to observe the petulant droop of
Amanda's mouth when all the nominations had been
confirmed.

Her only verbal objection to Christy's appointment
had been a pouted, 'Dominic, there was really no need
to involve Miss Marsden. I'm sure that my godmother's social secretary would have been more than
pleased to handle all the details. She is terribly
experienced at that sort of thing. She organised my
coming out ball and the wedding.'

'That's very kind of you, Amanda,' was Dominic's
diplomatic reply, 'but it would hardly be fair of us to
deprive your godmother of her secretary, especially
since we couldn't afford to pay for her services.'

The meeting broke up a little later than Christy had expected. They were the last to leave because she had to collect the plates from the kitchen, and she wanted to wash them first.

As she had dreaded that he might do, she heard her father inviting Dominic back for supper. Her body tensed as she waited to hear his acceptance, and then went stiffer still when he said apologetically, 'I'm afraid I can't tonight. I've already agreed to dine with Lady Anthony and Amanda.' He glanced at his watch as he spoke, and Christy felt a furious stab of resentment that he should make it so obvious that he was anxious for them to leave—a resentment that was entirely on her father's behalf, she assured herself, as she picked up her plates.

'We'll leave you to get ready for your date then, Dominic.' She gave him a smile as icy as her words. 'I should hate you to have to keep Amanda waiting on our behalf.'

Of course, once they got home, her mother wanted to hear about everything that had gone on.

'You're supposed to be resting,' Christy scolded her, but nevertheless, she made three mugs of coffee and took them upstairs on a tray together with some of the scones she had baked. Perching on the side of her mother's bed, she told her about the evening.

'Lady Anthony's god-daughter,' Mrs Marsden murmured at one point. 'Oh, yes, Dominic said that she was staying at the Manor. What's she like? Dominic said that she'd recently gone through a rather bad divorce.'

Recalling the animosity and the innate coldness she

had sensed in the other woman, Christy lifted her eyebrows a little.

'She's very attractive—brunette and petite—but she and I didn't exactly take to one another.'

'Of course not,' her mother agreed. 'She wants Dominic, and she'll have heard all about how close the pair of you used to be. She's bound to be resentful of the fact that you've come home.' She saw Christy's face, and it was her turn for her eyebrows to lift in surprised amusement. 'Oh, come on, Christy love, you're not that naïve,' she teased. 'You and Dominic *were* very close at one time. We live in a very enclosed community round here; you can hardly expect that there weren't those who, shall we say, wondered out loud whether your childhood friendship might lead to something closer?'

'You mean people gossiped about us,' Christy put in bitterly.

'If you want to put it like that, but it was never unkind gossip. It's only natural that people should be interested in one another. Dominic and his family are very popular around here, and I personally always thought there was something rather noble and endearing about the way he allowed you to follow him around. It can't have been easy for him at times, especially in the early days, when he was only a teenager himself.'

'Well, Amanda has no need to feel jealous or resentful towards me. Dominic and I are both adults now.'

'Mmm . . . perhaps that's what she's afraid of,' her mother commented cryptically, but she wouldn't be pressed into giving Christy an explanation of her remark. Not that Christy needed one. It was as clear as though she had spelled it out for her. As adults, she and Dominic were now both free to pursue the sort of relationship they could never have had before. The eight years that separated them meant nothing now.

But far more than mere age held them apart, and always would do, and despite the local romantic imaginings, she and Dominic would never be more than distantly polite enemies.

She changed the subject, telling her mother about the potential site for the new health centre that they were going to see, and asking her what she thought about her idea for the masked ball.

'I think it's an excellent one,' she told her promptly. 'So romantic . . .'

'That's what the Major said.' They both giggled as Christy repeated the Major's reaction to her proposals, the atmosphere lightening a little.

'Poor man; he's never married, you know, and he's the type who probably cherishes some impossibly romantic idea of a girl who never even knew that he cared about her. He's one of these old-fashioned true gentlemen who don't seem to exist any more.'

'Rather like Lady Anthony. She's another anachronism in many ways.'

'Mmm . . . They're very much of an age, as well.' Her mother yawned hugely, and Christy, remembering that she was still supposed to be recuperating, got up off the bed hastily.

'I'm tiring you, and you're supposed to be resting. I'm tired myself, as a matter of fact. I think I'll have an early night.'

She was tired, but not so tired that she didn't

wonder as she lay in bed how Dominic was enjoying himself with Amanda. A queer, bitter little pain seemed to come out of nowhere and curled itself around her heart. A funny pain that had no logical explanation, and which because of its very lack of logicality worried her even more.

CHAPTER FOUR

'I'M sorry, my dear, but you know what these farmers are like. If Harry Forbes says he wants to talk to me about his will this afternoon, then he means this afternoon or never. I'll have to go.'

'But we were supposed to be going to view these houses with the others,' exclaimed Christy, who had persuaded her father that she did not want to go alone.

'Well, *you* can still go. Give Dominic a ring, and tell him that you'll need a lift after all . . . or if you don't want to do that, you can always take your mother's car,' her father added diplomatically, seeing the look on her face. 'The roads are still slightly icy, though, and you'll have to take care. I shouldn't be surprised if we have more snow before the month's out.'

Given the choice of lowering her pride and begging Dominic for a lift or driving her mother's car, there was really only one option she could go for, Christy thought acidly. It would have to be her mother's car. It was just her luck that her father should get called away urgently like this, but there was absolutely nothing she could do about it.

Knowing that because of his detour to pick up Lady Anthony and Amanda, Dominic would have to set out early, Christy waited until she had seen his car go down the lane before she went out to the garage that housed her mother's small Renault.

Luckily the car started first time, and was relatively

easy to handle. Even so, she took extra care as she drove down the lane, dreading the sensation of feeling control of the vehicle slide away from her.

It was bitterly cold day, with an east wind blowing that could have cut glass. The sky was grey with lowering clouds, and she was glad that she had brought along the hooded fox jacket that David and Meryl had given her the previous year as a Christmas present. She glanced at it as she negotiated the narrow streets of Setondale. She should have guessed then what David had had in mind. It was a very extravagant gift for a mere assistant, no matter how highly thought of, but although the gift had surprised her, it had never occurred to her that it was to be the prelude to David's covert courtship.

She found the houses easily enough and parked the Renault at the side of the road, huddling into the fur before getting out. For comfort she had worn a pair of stretch cords in a soft butterscotch colour, and chestnut brown boots she had bought in a sale from a shop on Bond Street. The amber-gold pelts of her jacket, its hood pulled up against the wind, set off her creamy redhead's skin to perfection. Shivering in the icy blast, Christy locked the car, and curled her hands into her pockets before hurrying towards the buildings.

The Major, John Howard and Peter Bryant were already there, and greeted her with varying degrees of warmth as she explained her father's absence.

'A solicitor who's prepared to work on a Sunday, eh?' Peter Bryant commented. 'Sounds like a man after my own heart. I shall have to see if we can't put some of my business his way, eh, John?' Peter Bryant

was looking at her in a way she had learned to
recognise during her years in London, but she fielded
it with a pleasantly distancing smile and stepped back
from him, straight into Dominic, although when she
first felt the wall of solid muscle against her back she
had no idea who he was.

She whirled round in instinctive shock, the words of
apology dying on her lips.

The wind caught her hood and blew it back, her hair
tangling wildly round her face. She lifted an impatient
hand to push it away, and found she was standing so
close to Dominic that one more step would have
brought their bodies into physical contact. Beyond
him she could see Lady Anthony and Amanda, the
latter glaring at her with compressed lips and icy eyes.
Christy told herself that it was the cold that was
making her shiver so much, her balance suddenly
ridiculously insecure.

'Are you OK?'

Even through the warmth of her coat she could feel
the pressure of his fingers on her arm, steadying her.

She took a deep lungful of air and nearly choked on
it. For some reason it was impossible for her to meet
his eyes, and equally impossible for her to drag her
own away from his face. He had cut himself slightly
shaving, and her fingers itched to touch the small
wound. Her mouth had gone terribly dry. She licked
her lips nervously, instinctively shielding her eyes
from him by dropping her lashes.

'That's a beautiful jacket you're wearing, Christy.'

Thankfully Christy stepped back from him as Lady
Anthony's voice broke the spell that had held her

transfixed to the ground. 'Yes ... yes ... it was a present.'

'From your parents?' Amanda questioned with what Christy thought was rather rude curiosity.

Always brought up to be honest, it was impossible for her not to say, 'No ... no, actually I was given it by my ex-boss ...'

'And his wife,' she had been about to say, but she wasn't given any opportunity to do so, because Amanda's sharp blue eyes had rounded spitefully and before Christy could finish her sentence she was saying, 'My goodness, he must have thought an awful lot about you! Of course one hears about bosses who buy their secretaries fur coats, but I always thought they were just a joke.'

There was a small unpleasant silence, when Christy would have given the world not to have to look into Dominic's face. She read the condemnation in his eyes with a kind of sick awareness of what he was thinking, that was in no way mitigated by her own knowledge that he was wrong. What made it worse was that Amanda's unpleasant allegation had at least some basis for truth. David *had* wanted to make her his mistress, but she had been too naïve to realise it, until, at least as far as her jacket went, it was too late to do anything about it. Perhaps if she hadn't worked so much overtime that autumn she might have queried the expense of such a lavish gift, but David and Meryl were both extravagantly generous, and so she had simply accepted the gift at face value.

But she could hardly explain all of this to Dominic, and anyway, why should she want to? she asked wrathfully of herself as she stepped away from him and went over to join the others, who hadn't heard their conversation. What on earth did it matter to her what Dominic Savage thought of her?

'Dominic, let's get inside, it's freezing out here.' Slipping her hand through his arm, Amanda swept past Christy's motionless figure with a triumphant smile.

Once they were inside the house, Christy put Dominic out of her mind and tried to concentrate on her role as note-taker. She had brought her notebook with her, and listened attentively as Dominic explained his plans for the two buildings.

'It would be impossible for us to do everything we wanted to do all at once, but the scope is here. There is over half an acre of land with these houses, enough for a car park and extensions.'

They toured both houses from top to bottom while Christy made notes. Dominic knew exactly what he wanted and had the knack of putting it across in a way that the layman could easily understand, and almost against her will Christy found herself being fired with some of his enthusiasm for his project. There was no doubt that it was a worthwhile one, and the others evidently thought so too.

Busy with her notes, Christy didn't realise that she and Dominic were alone in one of the rooms until she glanced up and saw him watching her with a curiously pensive, almost brooding expression.

'He must know you very well to have chosen this for you.' His fingers reached out and touched the soft fur of her jacket. 'I'd never thought you'd grow up to be the sort of woman who would be content playing second fiddle, Christy. I thought you'd have too much pride.'

Her teeth ached from the strain of stopping herself from telling him that he was wrong and that she and David weren't lovers. But he was right about one thing: she did have too much pride—far too much to make any explanations to *any* man—and *especially* to him.

'Ah, there you are, Nicky darling. My godmother is ready to leave. You must stay and dine with us. I'm simply fascinated by what you're planning to do here, although really you're wasted in a small place like this. You should be practising in Harley Street.'

Chattering animatedly, Amanda led him away. Despite her fur jacket she was feeling intensely cold—too cold, Christy thought, shivering with a mixture of shock and outrage. Her fur embraced her body like a shroud—like a prison!—condemning her, and suddenly she felt as though she loathed it.

In point of fact Dominic had been wrong about one thing. Meryl had chosen the colour, not David. He had told her later that he had wanted to buy her a lynx dyed jacket, all white with spots of gold, but Meryl had protested that with her vivid colouring Christy should have the red.

Tiredly she followed the others outside. The temperature seemed to have dropped even further, and already it was dark. She unlocked the car door and slid inside starting the engine. Dominic's car had already gone.

She drove home slowly, wound up with a nervous tension that affected her ability to give all her attention to what she was doing. She turned into the lane and sighed with relief, only to feel the breath lock in her throat as the car wheel spun savagely out of control and, as though it had been wrenched from her hands by an unseen grip, the steering wheel seemed to develop a mind of its own and the car careered off the road and plunged down into a ditch.

It took her several minutes to realise what had happened, and then what seemed like another lifetime to struggle with the seat belt in a vain attempt to free herself. Horrible images of cars bursting into flames tormented her mind, and then, shockingly, the door was wrenched open and hard hands were reaching for her, unlocking the tangled seat belt and dragging her out of the car.

She looked up at her rescuer hazily, unable to differentiate between hallucinations and reality, his name leaving her lips on a husky whisper.

'Dominic, what . . .?'

'Don't try to talk, not just now.' His hands moved expertly over her body, clinically exact in their movements, and only when he had assured himself that nothing was damaged did some of his tension seem to relax.

'The car skidded . . . I . . .'

'I know what happened.' His voice sounded terse. 'I was right behind you. My God . . . You haven't broken anything, at least. Did you hit your head at all?'

'No . . . No, I don't think so.'

'I'll take you back to my place, and check you over properly . . .'

'No, I want to go home,'

'Looking like that?' His voice was scathing. 'What

do you think it's going to do to your mother if you walk in looking the way you do right now?'

She glanced down at herself in bewilderment and then lifted her eyes to meet his.

'Don't argue with me, Christy.'

'But the car . . .'

'I'll arrange for the garage to come and collect it. Now come on, let's get out of this damned wind.'

She made to walk, her breathing suspended as he swore under his breath and lunged forward, picking her up as easily as though she weighed next to nothing.

'Dominic . . .'

'Save it,' he advised her tersely.

His car was parked only yards away from her own, slewed across the road as though he had stopped abruptly. He opened the rear door and bundled her on to the back seat. She looked over his shoulder and saw that it had begun to snow.

'It's snowing.' Her mind seemed to be clogged with cotton wool, making it impossible for her to do more than utter the merest banalities.

'So it is.'

She could understand why he sounded so sarcastic, but that didn't stop the tears burning against the back of her throat. She was suffering from shock, she told herself, but the information didn't seem to penetrate past the barrier of pain lodged round her heart, and she shrank back from him as he leaned over her, much as she might have shrunk from a would-be attacker.

She heard him swear again and then the car door slammed.

She closed her eyes, willing herself not to burst into tears. The driver's door opened, the car rocking slightly as he got in. The engine purred into life, and she felt herself tensing as Dominic slipped it into gear. He was a far more able driver than she was herself, she acknowledged as the big car moved steadily over the icy lane.

She saw her father's car parked outside the house as they drove past, but Dominic made no attempt to stop and she felt too weak to protest. She could hear the gravel drive to the Vicarage crunching beneath the car wheels as they drove up it, and then the car stopped. She sat up and reached for the door handle.

'Leave it,' Dominic snapped, turning in his seat to frown bleakly at her. 'I don't want you putting any weight on your legs until I've checked you over properly. I'll carry you inside.'

Eight years ago Christy would have been delirious with delight at the thought of being in his arms. Now all she felt was apprehension, and a fine spear of pain that seemed to have no logical reason for springing into being.

'I thought you were supposed to be having supper at the Manor.'

As he bent to lift her out of the car she was overwhelmed by her own awareness of his proximity. A feeling of acute panic raced through her body and she had to force herself to breathe normally.

'Then you thought wrong, didn't you.' His abrupt tone warned her not to pursue the subject.

She could feel icy cold flakes of snow stinging her exposed skin as he carried her to the house. He paused to unlock the door, shifting her in his arms so that briefly her face rested against his neck. She could smell the warm male scent of his skin. Her body tensed

instantly against her awareness of him, her face drawn
into lines of rejection which he obviously mistook for
pain, as he pushed open the door and switched the
light on.

His 'What's wrong?' fanned a warm breath of air
against her skin, making her shiver wildly.

It wasn't possible for her to speak, only to shake her
head, denying that anything was the matter. Dominic
strode through into the library, and set her down on
the leather settee.

'Don't move from there, I'm going to go and ring
your father and explain what's happened. Then I'll
come back and check you over.'

Before he left, he knelt down and applied a lighted
match to the fire set in the grate. Christy watched the
flames spread and leap through the sticks and coal like
someone drugged as she waited for him to come back.
She was still suffering from shock, she told herself,
unwilling to admit that most of her shock was caused
not by the accident, but the proximity of Dominic, and
the realisation of what that proximity was doing to
her.

He came back within minutes, his face still grim.

'I've told your father that I don't think there's
anything to worry about, but for your mother's sake
we both think it best that you stay here this evening.
He's going to tell your mother that I invited you back
here for supper and that you accepted. If you go back
looking the way you do now, you're likely to cause her
to have a relapse.' He crouched down in front of her,
expertly sliding the zips down on her boots and
tugging them off before she could even think of a
protest. The heat of his palm as he held the arch of her

foot, his long fingers curling round her ankle, made her heart thud at twice its normal rate.

'You'll have to take these off, I'm afraid,' he told her, standing up and gesturing to her tight jeans.

Her face froze, and she knew suddenly and intensely that there was no way she could do what he asked. It was all very well to tell herself that he was a doctor, but he was also Dominic. She knew that she was being silly; after all, he had seen her growing up, a skinny, flat-chested, adoring child, but she wasn't that child any more, and for some reason she didn't want him looking at her body with that same clinical detachment with which he had studied it before.

'I'm perfectly all right.' To prove it she swung her legs to the floor and stood up, taking a few tentative steps, before she started to shiver and had to subside back on to the settee.

Far from being relieved, Dominic's mouth had compressed into a savagely inimical line.

'What is it, Christy?' he demanded harshly. 'Surely you aren't frightened of my taking advantage of the situation?'

The explicit way he let his glance linger on her body left her in no doubt as to what he meant. Even though she tried to suppress it, there was nothing she could do to control the hot surge of colour sweeping up under her skin.

'Don't be so ridiculous.' Her voice sounded unfamiliar and thick, almost as though it was choked with tears. She turned her head away from him and added huskily, 'I know quite well that you're the last person who'd ever want me, Dominic.'

She couldn't look at him, but even without doing so

she was intensely conscious of the stunned quality of his stillness. In the end she had to look at him, her eyes meeting the brilliant, disbelieving glitter of his in shocked astonishment.

'Is that what you honestly think?' He dropped down on to his heels and slid his hand into her hair so that she couldn't turn away from him. His voice sounded oddly rusty. 'Is it, Christy?'

She wanted to turn away from him, but there was no way she could. Instinctively she moistened her dry lips with the tip of her tongue, and then froze when she saw the way his eyes darkened and followed the movement.

'You've been pushing me away ever since you came home. I thought it was because . . .' he broke off and shook his head. The firelight danced on the exposed nape of his neck, and she had an aching desire to reach out and stroke it.

'Christy, what's gone wrong between us? What . . . ?'

She couldn't let herself listen to the husky seduction of his voice. He had hurt her once, and so badly that she had never really recovered. She *had* to remember that. She twisted beneath his hand and instantly he released her, his frown deepening.

'I don't know what game you think you're playing with me, Dominic,' she told him. 'You humiliated me once,' she burst out bitterly. 'I'm not going to let that happen again. It's all very well for you to act as though it never happened . . . as though you never virtually called me a little tramp . . .' Her colour was high now, her eyes glittering with unshed tears, her mind sliding back to the past, and her body shivering with pain.

Her voice broke, and because she knew she wasn't far from tears, she curled her hands into tight fists, willing herself not to give way, her face turned into the darkness of the settee and away from Dominic's probing scrutiny.

She heard him get up, and felt him standing in front of the fire, blocking off its warmth. He moved, almost restlessly, and then she heard him say, 'I'd no idea you felt like this. God in heaven, you *can't* be holding that against me, Christy! What was I supposed to do?' She felt him coming towards her and cringed back, but he didn't touch her, his voice roughening and coming from somewhere above. 'You were a child!' His voice was almost tortured now.

She struggled to sit up and face him, as he stood looking down at her.

'I was seventeen,' she told him bitterly.

'Like I said, just a child.'

She couldn't avoid the tight-lipped look he gave her or her shock as he suddenly swore savagely and volubly—something she had never before heard him do. 'A very provocative child, maybe,' he added tersely, 'but a child none the less.'

She was the one who should have been bitterly angry, not him. She couldn't understand that anger, and something of her lack of understanding must have shown in her face, for suddenly he grasped her shoulders and pulled her round into the firelight.

'You may be eight years older, Christy, but that doesn't seem to have made you any more mature. You've held on to your bitterness and resentment like a child instead of trying to see my point of view. What the devil was I supposed to do? What would you think of me right now, if I'd taken you up on your offer?'

It was something she had never thought of, and her eyes widened as he forced her to face up to the reality of what had happened between them. Now, as a woman of twenty-five herself, what *would* she think of a man of her own age who made love to an ignorant, adoring adolescent?

She shuddered as the realisation of what he had saved her from shot through her, falling back against the back of the settee like a jointless doll as he abruptly released her.

'You never even tried to see it from my point of view, did you?' He was pacing the floor now, his face in the shadows. 'My God, to think you've carried this resentment against me around with you all these years! I know I hurt and upset you, Christy, but I had to . . . can't you see that? I was so damned scared for you. You were such an innocent. Hell, you hadn't the faintest idea.' He broke off and swore again. 'I'm not in the right frame of mind to go into this right now. I'd no idea you felt like this.' He shook his head heavily like a man coming out of deep water for much-needed air.

Why did he keep on stressing that? It couldn't possibly matter to *him* what she thought.

Christy didn't realise she had spoken out loud until he caught hold of her again hauling her to her feet in front of him.

'Of *course* it damn well matters!' He was practically shouting at her. 'Do you believe for one moment that if you walked in here now and offered yourself to me like that I'd even think of turning you down?'

Shock crystallised inside her. She searched his eyes

and face for signs of mockery and saw only anguish and . . . and desire . . .

It was like being hit in the chest with an iron first. Dominic wanted her.

She opened her mouth and closed it again, and then heard him say in a thick, unfamiliar tone, through a haze of cotton-woolly disbelief, 'Do that again,' and her mouth opened instinctively to absorb the heat of his as he pulled her against him and kissed her with a famished kind of hunger that was so erotic that she had no defences against it.

Against her mouth she heard him mutter, 'You can't know how much I've wanted to do this. Even then, God help me. I want you, Christy. I want to take you upstairs to bed with me and make love to you until . . .'

It was his voice that brought her back to reality, making her pull away from him in panicky shock.

'What is it?'

She pushed him away, shaking her head, and as she did so, she saw him frown and look at her coat.

'I see. You're thinking of him. Is that it?' His mouth hardened and she saw the bitterness in his eyes. 'You'll have to forgive me. I forgot that you were committed . . . elsewhere.'

It would have been the easiest thing in the world for her to tell him how wrong he was, but some last shred of sanity luckily prevented her. He wanted her, he had said, and God alone knew she had wanted him. The moment his mouth touched hers she had known how much she ached and yearned for him; eight years of telling herself she had changed meant nothing. She had known the moment she felt his mouth against her own that she still loved him, but this time it was a woman's love, not a child's.

Half of her couldn't believe it—didn't want to believe it, but it was true none the less. She had to fight to keep back the hysterical laughter building up inside her.

'I'd better take you home.'

She didn't protest, simply allowing him to lead her to the front door, her mouth still tingling from the pressure of his kiss. Her body ached in a way that was far more intense than any mild desire that David had ever aroused in her.

How ironic fate could be. Almost she could laugh at the ridiculous folly of Dominic thinking that David was her lover, but just as long as he continued to think that, she was safe. If he ever discovered that no man had ever touched her, that no man had ever aroused the need in her that he could arouse, then she was lost. Lost because he would take her simply out of his own need and desire for her, and that was something she didn't think she could bear. Once, she had thought no further than the dazzling pleasure of having him make love to her, but then she had been a child convinced that somehow once he had made love to her, he must love her. Now she was adult and knew better. Dominic had said nothing about loving her, and she didn't think she could endure giving herself to him knowing that while he was her whole life, she was nothing more to him than a woman whom he wanted.

He drove her home in silence, parking his car close enough to the door for her to get out and dash up to it, before he could join her.

'No, don't come in with me,' she told him fiercely as she unlocked the door, and to her relief he stepped back towards his car, leaving her to face her father's surprise at her early return on her own.

CHAPTER FIVE

CHRISTY was profoundly thankful to have the excuse of her mishap with the car to explain away her pallor and tension when she went upstairs to face her mother. The shock, not only of the discovery of her love for Dominic, but also of the anger he had exhibited when she had brought up the subject of their eight-year-old quarrel, were not things she could easily put out of her mind.

Realising that her daughter was both upset and on edge, Sarah Marsden wisely refrained from questioning her at length, suggesting instead that she have an early night.

'You're the one who's supposed to be the invalid, not me,' Christy protested with a wan smile.

'I don't know. Your father said that Dominic sounded most concerned when he rang up. I must admit I expected you to come home in a far more battered and bruised state than you have.'

Her bruises were there all right, but they were all inside, Christy, reflected ruefully.

'Why didn't Dominic come in with you? He knows that he's always welcome.'

'Lady Anthony had invited him round for supper.' An invitation which he had originally refused.

'At her god-daughter's behest, no doubt. Dominic is a very attractive man.' She paused, almost as though expecting Christy to deny it, but she wasn't that good a liar. She got up off the bed, trembling slightly as she remembered the passion with which Dominic had kissed her. If Amanda had been the one in his arms, she doubted that the other woman would have run away from him like a frightened child. What was the matter with her? she asked herself crossly as she prepared for bed. She had done the right thing; the only thing in the circumstances. She loved him too much to settle for a brief affair, no matter how passionate.

For over a week she saw nothing of Dominic, and she told herself that she was glad. The snow her father had prophesied fell heavily one night, smothering the countryside in a soft white blanket. A fierce frost on top of the snow kept them virtually housebound, but Christy discovered, after the second occasion on which she deliberately kept out of the way when her mother was due for her daily visit from the doctor, that Dominic had as little desire to see her as she had him, because it was not he who called to see her mother, but his partner.

She had already typed up the notes she had taken at the committee meeting, and telephone calls from both the Major and Lady Anthony had confirmed that they were going ahead with their plans for the masked ball.

As soon as the weather conditions permitted, Christy went with her father to Newcastle and spent the morning in a small, dusty stationers, tucked away down a side street, where the proprietor had to move aside huge bundles of out-of-date legal stationery before he could find for her a book containing sample invitation cards. Bearing in mind the nature of the event, and the probable reaction of Amanda Hayes to anything she might choose, she deliberately decided on the largest and most formal card available and left her order with the shop. Her father, who had business of his own to conduct with a fellow solicitor in the city, had suggested that they have lunch together in a small restaurant that had always been one of her favourites as a child. It had changed hands several times since Christy had first dined in it, and the pretty soft peach and french blue décor chosen by the latest proprietors was very warming on such a cold and miserable day.

The building was an old one, and the proprietors had made the most of its low-ceilinged, beamed interior. A good fire burned in the grate, and when Christy gave her name, she was informed that her father had not yet arrived, and offered a comfortable seat in one of the huge leather chairs in the bar area.

She had just ordered a drink when the door opened and another couple came in. Her heart seemed to stand still, gripped in an intolerable vice of pain as she recognised Dominic and Amanda, the latter clinging possessively to Dominic's arm.

He looked at Christy without smiling, his eyes grim and forbidding. Tears rose up inside her, forcing her to look away, her bottom lip caught up in her small teeth. Her surroundings blurred dangerously as she looked frantically into the fire, willing her tears to subside. She couldn't break down in front of them like this. Dominic was right. She hadn't grown up; she was behaving in a way that would have disgraced an eighteen-year-old, never mind a woman of twenty-five.

'My goodness, what a small world,' Amanda commented in an affected drawl. 'But then, I suppose in such a backwater one has to expect to run into people one knows. Are you alone?'

Her disparaging glance suggested that she must be, and Christy had difficulty in summoning a voice polite enough to answer her.

'No, I'm waiting for my father. I came with him this morning so that I could order the invitations for the ball.'

'Oh, you should have left that to me. Mummy uses this marvellous man in London . . .'

The artificial voice grated on Christy's too-tender nerves. She told herself that there was something faintly ridiculous about a grown woman in her late twenties referring to her parent as 'Mummy'.

'Darling, I'm just dying for a drink,' Amanda continued. 'Something civilised. I'll let you choose for me. You know what I like.'

It took all her willpower for Christy not to look away as Amanda batted her eyelashes at Dominic. A little grimly she wondered when the other woman would realise that she was overdoing things a little and that Dominic was not in the least remotely interested in Christy herself. She would have thought that the cool way in which he had acknowledged her presence would have been enough. The look of rejection and dislike in his eyes had surely been explicit enough even for someone as patently dim as Amanda appeared to be.

While Dominic went over to the small bar, Amanda leaned forward maliciously. 'What do you plan to wear for the ball? I thought I might have something new made. My godmother suggested that I go to

David again . . . David Emanuel, that is. His designs
are simply super.'

Christy only just managed to bite back the tart
comment that there was absolutely no need for her to
underline the disparity in their financial and social
positions with such name-dropping. Fortunately,
before she could give rein to her acid thoughts,
Dominic was back. Without even having to look at
him, Christy was acutely conscious of him, and of the
way he chose to sit down on Amanda's far side—as far
away from *her* as possible. He had no need to
underline the fact that he wanted nothing more to do
with her, she thought wretchedly; that much was
already abundantly clear.

Since their last meeting she had had time to think
properly about what he had said to her, and to accept
the truth of his heated comments. Of course he could
not have made love to her; of course he had been
morally bound to turn her down; and of course now
she could understand why he had felt it so incumbent
upon him to frighten her with the reality of where her
foolishness might have led.

What perhaps both of them had underestimated
had been the intensity of her feelings for him.
Whereas she had no doubt now that he had only meant
to shake her into a realisation of what she was doing to
herself, he had actually instilled in her such an
intensity of doubt and self-loathing that he had
effectively paralysed her instinctive responses.

'I was just telling Christy that I'll have to go to
London to arrange to have a new gown made for the
ball.' Amanda pouted provocatively and smiled at
him. 'Why don't you come with me, darling? It will do

you good to have a break. You work far too hard.'

The despairing sickness inside her seemed to bloom
and grow as Christy was forced to listen to their
conversation. She turned away, not wanting to hear
Dominic's reply, so thoroughly relieved to see her
father walk into the restaurant that she almost spilled
her drink as she got up to greet him.

'Hello, Dominic. I didn't expect to see you here.'

'I had to come to Newcastle on business.'

'And I'm afraid I came with him to distract him,'
Amanda cooed. Christy could see that it was on the tip
of her father's tongue to suggest that they all lunched
together, and she knew that to watch Amanda flirting
with Dominic over the lunch table was more than she
could endure. She had always been blessed with a
particularly vivid imagination, and she didn't need
any prompting from Amanda to guess that the two of
them were lovers. A man with the strong sexual drive
she had sensed when Dominic had kissed her would
not deny himself the company of an attractive and
willing woman for very long—and why should he?

'Dad . . . if you don't mind, I'd rather go straight
home than eat. I'm not . . . I'm not terribly hungry.'

She didn't care any more how betraying her
admission might be. She didn't even care about the
level, glinting look Dominic gave her as she turned to
plead with her father. All she cared about was getting
out of the intimate, pretty atmosphere of the restaurant and escaping from the knowledge that being
in the same room as Dominic at this particular
moment in time was more than she could bear.

She saw her father frown, but as though he sensed
her desperation he agreed calmly, 'Well, if that's what

you want . . . I must admit I'm never too happy about leaving your mother for very long.'

He went across to explain the change in plans to the owner, and paid for Christy's drink, and as they walked out into the raw, cold afternoon Christy wondered a little at the savagely comprehensive contempt she had seen in Dominic's eyes as he watched her go.

'Phone call for you, Christy.'

Her heart thumped as she walked through into the hall. She had told herself she was behaving crazily, and that Dominic was hardly likely to be telephoning her, especially since she knew from seeing him in Newcastle three days ago that he was obviously dating Amanda, but even so, the flutters in her stomach didn't settle until she spoke into the receiver and heard Meryl's familiar voice answering her.

'Meryl! But . . .'

'I'm sorry to disturb you, Christy, but I desperately need your help. David is due to fly out to Hollywood in a couple of days, and you know what he's like. It's panic, panic, panic, and now I can't seem to find the manuscript for *Fathers and Daughters*. He swears that it should be filed with all the others, but it isn't there, and you know how impossible he can be when he gets into one of his moods. He wants to take it with him, because it seems the Americans might be interested, and you're my last hope.'

In spite of her own misery Christy grinned to herself. David's methods of filing were notorious, as were the moods he flew into whenever anyone dared to criticise or complain about his lack of proper methods.

'Well, I can't think of anywhere offhand. Have you tried the pending file? Or the one marked "M"?'

'M?' Meryl queried.

'For mistakes,' Christy informed her with another grin.

'I've looked everywhere, and I'm at my wits' end.'

She sounded it, and Christy felt a surge of sympathy for her.

'Look, I know it's an awful imposition, but I was wondering if you could possibly come down. We could put you up overnight, and you could go through the files with me. You know what a calming effect you always have on David. At this moment in time I'd happily file him under "M" myself. "M" for monster,' she added feelingly.

'Oh, Meryl, I'm afraid I can't.'

There was an unhappy silence that made her feel extremely uncomfortable, and then her father, who had walked out into the hall queried, 'Can't what?'

'Can't go to London,' Christy told him, covering the receiver. 'Meryl can't find one of David's plays, and she wanted me to go down there and give her a hand.'

'Nonsense. Of course you can go. Do you good, if you ask me,' her father added vigorously. 'You need a break. Besides, you'll be able to get yourself something for this Grand Ball.'

Christy frowned. She could hardly explain to her father or to Meryl why she didn't want to see David again. She gnawed at her bottom lip and then heard Meryl asking anxiously if they had been cut off.

'No . . . no, I'm still here.'

'Look, Christy, I hate to pressure you, but I really do need your help. You've no idea what it's like down here! David is driving me mad . . . and besides . . .' her voice seemed to fade away a little and then rallied again as she said with a false brightness that cut Christy to the heart, 'I don't need to pretend with you. I suspect that he's deep in the throes of a new affair, and it's making him more unbearable than ever.'

While her heart went out to Meryl, Christy couldn't help thinking that if she was right—and Meryl knew her husband very well indeed—then she herself need have no fears about seeing David.

'Well, if you really need me . . .'

'Oh, you're a darling! When can you come?'

Before she hung up it was arranged that Christy would catch the early morning train from Newcastle the following day, and that she would stay overnight with her old employers before returning home. She was touched almost to tears that evening when her father called her into his study, and after much indecision presented her with an extremely generous cheque which he told her she was to use to buy herself a ballgown. When she protested at his generosity, reminding him feelingly that she had already caused him expense by damaging her mother's car, he told her not to be so silly, adding bracingly, 'Besides, you've got the honour of Setondale to uphold, you know. Can't have our local girl being outshone by an incomer!'

Christy laughed, but she didn't have the heart to tell her parent that, generous though his cheque was, it would hardly buy her a dress that could compete with the Emanuel outfit with which Amanda was planning to dazzle them.

To save her father having to get up early, she ordered a taxi to take her to Newcastle for the early morning train. When her alarm went off at four, she groaned, and went through the motions of getting washed and dressed, feeling like a zombie. She didn't feel much better when she eventually got on the train and eschewed the dining car, to curl up and catch up on her shortened sleep in the comfort of her seat in the first class section. It was a welcome surprise to discover that Meryl had come to the station to meet her.

'You shouldn't have bothered,' Christy protested, when she had disengaged herself from her welcoming hug. 'I could easily have made my own way to Wimbledon, and you must have a hundred and one things to do.'

'A thousand and one,' Meryl agreed ruefully, 'but I needed the luxury of a familiar shoulder to cry on.' She acknowledged Christy's comprehensive look with a wry smile. 'Oh, don't feel sorry for me; after all, I stay with him by choice, but there are times when I wonder if I'm just a fool, or a masochist. I tell myself that deep down there somewhere he loves me.'

She grimaced slightly as Christy interrupted fiercely, 'He does, Meryl. I know he does.'

'I wonder. That's what I've always told myself, but now I'm beginning to wonder. It wouldn't be so bad if the others all shared your moral code, Christy.' She saw her start with surprise and allowed herself a grim smile.

'Oh, I might be stupid, but I'm not dense. Women

like me with wandering husbands soon learn to
recognise the signs. I must admit that with you it took
a bit longer than usual. It was when he wanted to buy
you that fox that the truth dawned.'

'But you still . . .'

'I chose it for you because it was a present that you
richly deserved. I must admit that for a while I
wondered if you'd be able to resist him. In fact, I
couldn't see how you could. He can be very persuasive
when he wants to be . . . but when you said you were
going to resign I knew then that I had nothing to worry
about from you.'

Christy saw the tears standing out in Meryl's eyes
and cursed David for his insensitivity. Never had she
been more glad that she hadn't given in to the physical
impulse to take David as her lover. She could never
have faced the grief and torment in Meryl's eyes if she
had.

'Oh, and I promised myself I wouldn't behave like
this. It's just that . . .' Meryl broke off, and as Christy
looked at her she realised that she had put on weight,
and that she was moving less briskly than usual.

Meryl watched her and then said tiredly, 'Yes,
ridiculous, isn't it, at my age? And what on earth
David will say I don't know. At the moment he thinks
I've just been indulging in a bout of over-eating, and I
want him to go on thinking that way, at least until
we're all safely established in Hollywood. If I tell him
that I'm pregnant now, he'll seize on that as an excuse
to leave me behind. And we all know what happens to
wives who get left behind, don't we? A temporary
separation all too often becomes a permanent one.'

'You're having a baby!'

'Thanks,' Meryl said drily. 'You're doing wonders for my ego.'

'Oh no, I didn't mean it that way . . .'

'No . . . I know. It came as something of a shock to me as well, I can tell you,' Meryl confided, leading the way to her parked car. 'To say nothing of what it's going to do to David. It was a genuine accident, but remember—not a word to him.'

The traffic was very heavy and Christy didn't try to distract her companion by trying to talk to her, but at last they were out of the city and heading for the Galvins' comfortable house in Wimbledon.

'David's out, and the kids are at school,' Meryl told her as she unlocked the front door and led the way into the comfortable study that David worked in. 'He stormed out in something of a huff. No doubt he's gone round to see Mirabelle Hastings for sympathy and comfort.'

There was an edge of bitterness to her voice that Christy wasn't used to hearing. 'He'll get tired of her eventually, Meryl.'

'Yes, I know. He always does. But what I'm not sure about any longer is whether I've got the resilience to make myself wait. I always used to tell myself that I was lucky to be married to a man like David, and that because he *is* the man he is I must just pay the price that being married to such a man demands, but just lately I'm beginning to wonder if I wouldn't have been better off married to someone else—someone who puts me first and not himself.'

Christy looked at her in consternation. 'Meryl . . .'

'Oh, don't take any notice of me. It must be this baby. Come on, help me to find this damned script. I'll go and tell Helga to make us some coffee.'

Helga was the latest in a long line of au pairs and while Meryl went off to find her, Christy started to go through the files.

It took them two hours to find the missing script; jammed in between two files, it had slipped to the bottom of the drawer.

'Between "G" and "H",' Meryl said in disgust. 'What on earth was it doing there?'

'God alone knows . . . or, more probably, David alone,' Christy said ruefully, being perfectly acquainted with her late boss's habit of pushing unwanted documents anywhere and everywhere simply to get them off the top of his desk.

'Well, that's that, then,' Meryl flopped into a chair. 'You must be cursing me for dragging you all this way simply to find this . . .'

'No, it's all right. I had to come to London anyway. I need a ballgown.'

More to distract Meryl than because she was actually worried about finding something to wear, Christy told her of Dominic's plans to open the new health centre, and more particularly of her own involvement in it.

'No, you mustn't bother to go out and buy anything,' Meryl told her. 'What you ought to do is to hire something. Use one of the theatrical agencies. They have the most fabulous outfits.'

Meryl was right, Christy recognised. She gnawed anxiously at her bottom lip. 'I thought you had to be a member of Equity at the very least to hire anything from one of those places.'

'Being David's wife has some advantages,' Meryl

told her darkly. 'I know the very place. I hired an
outfit from them for the Palfrys' New Year do. It was
fabulous. Come on, I'll give them a ring and then we'll
go straight round.'

Sensing that Meryl needed to keep busy to keep her
mind off her husband, Christy allowed herself to be
persuaded.

Within an hour she was being shown an abundance
of ballgowns that would even have silenced Amanda.

'How about this one?' the woman in charge
suggested, lifting a glowing off-white satin number
with the colour and sheen of mother-of-pearl off its
protective hanger. 'It was designed for Kate in the
Shrew—perfect for a redhead with your creamy skin.'

Enviously Christy stroked the supple fabric, wondering how on earth the designers had managed to
achieve that unearthly opalescent effect. The low-cut
bodice was encrusted with pearls, the bodice dipping
to a sharp V at the front, from which the full skirts
frothed out in true Elizabethan grandeur.

'Try it on,' Meryl urged.

Christy needed the help of the assistant to get the
dress fastened up the back. The bodice clung to her
like a second skin, the whaleboning causing her
breasts to swell against the tight fabric. When she
remarked on this the assistant shook her head. 'That's
the way it's meant to be. It's a perfect fit on you, and
the length is right as well.'

At Meryl's behest she went outside to show her.

'It's fabulous, Christy, you must have it.'

'I'll need a mask,' Christy warned her, allowing
herself to be tempted. Hire of the gown would be

expensive, but nothing like as expensive as buying a new one.

'A mask—I've got the very thing,' the assistant told her. 'This gown was designed for a ball scene as it happens—a little addition the producer of this particular version of the *Shrew* wanted, and there just happens to be a mask to go with it.'

'There you are,' Meryl exclaimed with a grin. 'It was quite obviously meant to be.'

The mask was in the same satin as the dress and trimmed lavishly with pearls. It gave Christy's face a curiously fey and unreal dimension, somehow making her mouth look fuller and exaggerating the oval slant of her eyes.

'It's perfect,' Meryl told her, adding to the assistant, 'we'll take it.'

While the gown was being packed up Christy had a peep at some of the others hanging in the same closet. There were ballgowns from every era imaginable: brief wisps of Regency chiffon, crystal-beaded twenties shimmies, elegant *belle époque* bustles.

'You could spend a lifetime here, couldn't you?' asked Meryl, drooling over a Fortuny pleated hank of silk chiffon.

David's car was parked in the drive when they got back, and instantly Christy was aware of the change in Meryl. She seemed to close up and withdraw into herself, and Christy's heart ached for her friend.

'There you are, Meryl; where the devil have you been? You know we're due to attend tonight's performance.' David's irritable voice broke off as he saw Christy standing at his wife's side. In the shadows of the hallway, Christy saw him flush slightly as though he was suddenly aware of how unpleasant he was being to Meryl.

'Christy, my love . . . what are you doing here?' He made no attempt to embrace her.

'I asked Christy to come down to help me look for your manuscript,' Meryl told him.

Christy watched as he shifted uncomfortably from one foot to the other. 'We found it filed between "G" and "H",' she told him drily. He had the grace to look faintly shamefaced.

'I suppose I've been a bit of a bear lately . . . it's all this business about going to the States.'

'Oh, really? I thought it was something else you had on your mind.'

Christy wasn't sure which of them was the more surprised. David was watching his wife's retreating back with his mouth agape. It was so unusual for Meryl to say anything even slightly contentious to her husband that none of them seemed to know quite what to say.

It was only when she had disappeared into the kitchen that David relaxed a little, expelling his breath and swearing slightly. 'I don't know what the devil's got into Meryl recently.'

'Don't you?' Christy asked him pointedly, looking at him.

'What the hell does that mean?' He was frowning and blustering as he always did when he knew himself to be in the wrong, and there was certainly nothing even remotely lover-like in the way he gripped her arm and almost dragged her into his study.

'Just what's going on around here?' he demanded, growling at her. 'Meryl's been unliveable-with these last few weeks. Not her normal self at all.'

'Perhaps she's just getting tired of a husband who's consistently unfaithful to her,' Christy suggested tartly, and then instantly wished her hasty words unsaid. It was no business of hers, and Meryl would probably not thank her for interfering.

'You mean she knows? She's told you?'

For an intelligent man he could be exceedingly dense. Christy gave him an ironic look.

'She's always known, David,' she told him. 'It's just that in the past she's chosen to turn a blind eye. Why do you think I wouldn't have an affair with you?' she mocked him gently. 'Not because I wasn't tempted.' She could almost have laughed at the way he preened himself. 'You're a very attractive and dangerously persuasive man when you want to be, but Meryl is my friend. I care for her too much to hurt her for what would have at best been only a very brief physical fling.'

'You do have a way of bringing a man down to earth, don't you?' David commented wryly, and she could tell that even though he was amused he was also a little shocked by her outspokenness.

'Oh, come on. What do you expect, David? I've worked for you for too long to have any illusions. A new face comes along, you convince yourself that you've fallen in love, but once the excitement of the chase is over, it's back to reality and Meryl. Have you ever thought what would happen if she wasn't there to go back to?'

It was plain to Christy that he hadn't. He stood there frowning down at her, looking as hurt and puzzled as a small child.

'But she'll always be there. She's . . . she's part of me.'

'Will she?' Christy asked him wryly, and watched the doubts shimmer in his dark eyes.

'She loves you, David,' she told him softly, 'but love doesn't always last for ever.'

He swallowed and looked at her with shocked eyes.

'Are you trying to tell me that Meryl's found someone else?' He seemed to look past her and stare into space. 'She *has* been different lately. That would explain . . .' He gave her a brooding look and Christy said hastily,

'She hasn't said that to me, but I do know that she's unhappy.'

'Meryl, unhappy?'

He looked so affronted that if it hadn't been so serious Christy could almost have laughed.

She had interfered enough—perhaps even too much, she told herself as David turned away to glare through the window with brooding intensity. For herself, she didn't doubt that he loved his wife—she had *never* doubted it—but Meryl needed and deserved more than David was giving her, and it would do him no harm to think that he might lose her.

Whatever the outcome of her interference, at least she knew one thing, and that was that David's feelings for her were once again simply those of a friend. She hadn't ever really feared that he would pursue her to the Borders; there were too many more easily accessible distractions in his life for that, but it was still a relief to know that his pursuit of her was over.

Later in the evening, she was a little surprised by the firmness with which Meryl refused to accompany

David to the theatre.

'It will do him good to be turned down once in a while. His lady love isn't on stage tonight. Her understudy is taking the part, so he won't have the consolation of watching her. I suspect that's why he wanted me to go, but for once I decided I wasn't prepared to play second fiddle.' Her face changed all of a sudden, crumbling. 'Oh God, Christy, I'm such a fool. Why on earth don't I simply give up? I *can't* go on competing . . .'

'You don't need to. He does love you, Meryl. I just think he needs to be reminded how much occasionally. He'll never change. He'll always be a terrible flirt, but if you could have seen his face this afternoon when I suggested to him that you might be tired of him.'

Meryl stared at her. 'You said that . . .'

'Umm . . . and David looked as shocked as a child being told that there isn't any Father Christmas.'

'Mmm. I never thought of trying to make him jealous.'

Christy grinned. 'Well, I shouldn't throw yourself too energetically into the part.' She looked meaningfully at Meryl's stomach. 'With David's vivid imagination . . .'

'Oh God, yes. Well, maybe I'll save that for next time. After junior has safely arrived. After all, we can't give David too many shocks all at once!'

They both laughed, and Christy was pleased to see how much more cheerful Meryl looked. Both of them were surprised when David came home early, but Christy tactfully took herself off to bed, claiming that the unaccustomed pace of London life had exhausted her.

CHAPTER SIX

'WELL, there you are, safely delivered, and on time.'
With cheerful disregard for the fact that he was
occupying a space reserved for taxis, David slid his
Ferrari into the kerb. Ahead of them a taxi was
disgorging its passenger, and Christy felt her stomach
jerk as though she had suddenly ascended ten floors in
a high-speed lift, as she recognised Dominic's dark
head and lean body emerging from its interior.

As though by some alchemy that was beyond
rational analysis, he turned his head and looked
straight at her. She had no need to possess any mind-
reading gift to interpret the hard contempt in his eyes
as his glance raked from her to David.

While she was staring back at him in hypnotised
agony David leaned across her, oblivious to what was
happening, and kissed her full on the mouth. It wasn't
a lover's kiss, merely the exuberant embrace of a man
who enjoyed kissing women and who knew without
conceit that they enjoyed it too, and Christy detached
herself from it with ease, but when she looked towards
the taxi, Dominic had gone.

Of course David insisted on going with her to the
barrier, carrying the box with her dress in it, and
kissing her again. This time on the cheek.

'Have a safe journey back. You'll have to fly out and
see us when we're in the States.'

As she hurried on to the train Christy searched the

first class compartments hoping to avoid any sight of
Dominic. And where was Amanda? By what malig-
nant turn of fate had she chosen to come down to
London at exactly the same time as they did? Her face
burned suddenly as she thought of the construction
Dominic might have put on her appearance, but then
she relaxed as she remembered that he had also seen
her with David, and there had been no doubt from his
expression what interpretation he had put on *that*. No,
he could hardly think she was following *him* after
witnessing that kiss, thank goodness!

She settled herself comfortably in her seat, wishing
she had had the forethought to get some magazines,
but David had bustled her on to the train without
giving her the chance to buy any. She turned her face
towards the window as the train started to move. She
hoped that things would work out for Meryl and
David. She liked them both, but she had a special
fondness and sympathy for Meryl.

Lost in thought, she was aware of someone
subsiding into the seat next to hers.

Out of the corner of her eye she caught the brief
glimpse of sun-tanned lean wrist and immaculate shirt
cuff, and her stomach muscles suddenly clenched
protestingly in immediate recognition.

'Dominic!' His name had left her lips before she
could suppress it, and as she turned towards him, her
suspicions confirmed, she saw the contemptuous way
his mouth curled as he acknowledged her husky
whisper.

'Dreaming about your lover, were you?'

He didn't wait for her to confirm or deny his
allegation. 'Odd, isn't it, how easily we human beings

deceive ourselves? There was a time when I would have said you were the last person to involve yourself in a relationship with someone who was committed to someone else.'

His open contempt hurt and made her want to lash out at him to ease her pain.

'People change, Dominic,' she told him.

'So I'm beginning to realise.' He looked up and saw the box containing her dress on the parcel shelf above them. A cynical glitter darkened his eyes, and he reached up and touched the box with his fingertips, asking her dulcetly, 'What's this, Christy? Payment for services rendered, like the fur coat?'

She ached to hit out at him, conscious of the way her face was burning with a mixture of rage and pain.

She stood up, trembling with the force of her emotion, reaching for the box, and at the same time trying to scramble past him as she said fiercely, 'I don't need paying to spend time with the man I love.'

She couldn't get past him. His long legs were thrust out in front of him, and she couldn't seem to move without coming into physical contact with him.

Her voice thick with frustration, she demanded huskily, 'Dominic, please let me past.'

'Why?'

She turned and stared at him. There was a deceptively calm amusement in his eyes. She sucked in air, her muscles tensing. He was enjoying baiting her like this, and he had no intention of letting her go.

'Sit down, Christy,' he told her softly. 'You're creating a scene.' She looked round and saw that he was right—other travellers were beginning to stare at them. 'I've got my car at Newcastle, and my first appointment when I get home is to see your mother. She'll think it odd when she learns that we've travelled home on the same train without seeing one another.'

Christy knew that he was right, but there was no way she wanted to spend the journey fending off his acid comments.

'Where's Amanda?' she asked him curtly, subsiding back into her seat.

'Staying on in London with her mother for a few days.'

The look on his face prompted her into irrational retaliation for his cruel remarks to her. 'I'm surprised she allowed you to return without her,' she taunted, but instead of getting angry, he merely laughed, his eyes glittering with a strange intensity as he turned to her and whispered mockingly,

'Why, Christy, anyone would think you were jealous.'

He might have forced her to remain sitting with him, but she didn't have to talk to him, Christy told herself. Compressing her mouth, she turned away from him and stared out of the window. Already she could feel the tension invading her body. Her throat was dry and she ached for something to drink.

Quite how she managed to fall asleep she didn't know, but somehow she must have done, and it was the sound of Dominic's voice in her ear, and the pressure and heat of his torso pressed against hers as he leaned across to shake her, that finally made her wake up.

Totally disorientated, she stared mutely up at him, noticing for the first time that his eyes weren't a flat hard grey after all, and that there was a band of darker almost blue-black colour round the iris.

Fascinated, she stared at it, until the sound of his voice brought her back to reality, and she became intensely aware of the heat emanating from his body, and the rebellious response of her own to his proximity. Beneath her jacket she could feel the prickling awareness swelling her breasts. Nervously her glance dropped from his, unintentionally lingering on the sculptured hardness of his mouth. She felt herself start to tremble. What would it be like to trace that hard outline with her fingertips; to feel his mouth on hers? Sick with need and fear, she tensed back from him. Was it her imagination, or was there something dangerous about the thick, tense silence that seemed to engulf them?

She couldn't bring herself to look into Dominic's eyes and read for herself that he was aware of her self-betrayal.

'I've brought you a cup of coffee and a sandwich.'

The mundaneness of the words calmed her frantic imaginings, and she forced a polite smile to her lips— lips that suddenly seemed stiff and unwilling to move as ordered by her brain.

What a terrifyingly complex man Dominic was turning out to be. How could he change so quickly? Not an hour ago he had been berating and taunting her, and yet here he was now talking to her as calmly and pleasantly as he had done in the days when she was still a child, and he was her adored hero. But beneath that pleasant, almost lazily indulgent surface lurked dangers she as a child hadn't known existed, and consequently, although Dominic seemed to have abandoned his earlier aggression and talked

pleasantly to her, telling her about the years he had
spent in America, Christy was on her guard against
him, her responses stilted and slightly unnatural.

Every time he tried to turn the conversation in her
direction she instinctively parried every question,
refusing to allow him to draw her into any intimate
confidences. And yet, even as she did so, she was
painfully aware that in other circumstances she could
too easily have allowed herself to drift back into their
old relationship. He still exercised a power and
enchantment for her that she knew would never
entirely disappear, but then she suspected that few
women would be able to withstand Dominic if he
chose not to allow them to do so.

The train was drawing into Newcastle station when
she saw him frown, a derisory glitter darkening his
eyes as he scrutinised her.

'It isn't going to work, is it, Christy?' he taunted her
with a return to his earlier cynicism. 'There's no way
you and I can ever be polite acquaintances, is there?'

She felt as though her heart was being torn into
pieces, but she managed to say calmly enough, 'Is
there any reason why we should be?'

She saw his face darken. He turned away from her
as he muttered under his breath, 'No . . . no damned
reason at all,' and then he was lifting her dress box
down for her, and she had no alternative but to follow
him out of the train and along the station to his parked
car.

She told herself that she was glad of his silence as he
drove them home, but in truth it was more nerve-
racking than she wanted to admit. She couldn't stop
her foolish heart from imagining all manner of

romantic scenarios, in which instead of being two
people enduring an enforced intimacy as though it
were a penance, they were what she had always
dreamed they might be: two lovers inhabiting a
silence that sprang from perfect communion with one
another.

When he stopped outside her parents' home, he
spoke for the first time. 'I'll come in and see your
mother now.'

Of course her mother was delighted to see them
both, expressing delight and pleasure when she heard
they had travelled back from London together.

'And did you manage to sort out David's problem?'
she asked Christy while her father went downstairs to
make them all some coffee.

'Yes, we found the file.'

'And Meryl's well, is she?'

Sarah Marsden had heard all about David's wife
from Christy. 'Yes. Well, she's as well as can be
expected.' She had been staring out of the window
while Dominic pulled off his jacket, and now she
turned round to address her mother, her breath
catching in her throat as she saw the way the fine
cotton clung to his body. Beneath it she could see the
clear outline of his torso, and she stood, breathless and
aching with love for him as she watched the masculine
play of muscles and felt the need run through her body
in a white-hot searing tide.

'Christy . . .'

The plaintive note in her mother's voice brought her
back to reality and her unfinished sentence. Now her
face was as hot as her body had been seconds before.

'Er . . . yes . . . Meryl's pregnant.'

She was aware of a sharply indrawn breath, and only realised it was Dominic's when she glanced at him and saw the savage condemnation bracketing his mouth.

Too late she realised the interpretation he would put on her remark, and sure enough, as he came over to the bed, he stopped at her side to mutter bitterly in her ear, 'And you still accept him as your lover, knowing that? What sort of woman are you, Christy?'

The sort who's foolish enough to go on loving you even though my love isn't wanted, she longed to cry out, but the years of self-control stopped her.

Her father's arrival with the coffee broke into the unnatural silence. Dominic moved to her mother's side.

'Well, you seem to be making excellent progress,' he pronounced as he stood up.

'It's all this spoiling I'm getting,' Sarah smiled back at him. 'Which brings me to a favour I'd like to ask you, Dominic.'

Why on earth couldn't he smile at her like that . . . just once, Christy thought bitterly, instead of always thinking the worst of her?

Later she decided that her absorption in Dominic's smile had been the reason her intuition hadn't warned her what was coming, but by then it was too late.

'I was wondering if you would drive Christy to and from the ball,' her mother was saying. 'Tim doesn't want to go. He says it won't be any fun without me.' She gazed fondly across at her husband. 'And after . . .' she looked apologetically at Christy, 'well, after her slight mishap with the car we would be worried about her driving, especially if the weather is bad.'

For a moment Christy was too appalled to speak. She couldn't look at Dominic, and then, her tongue suddenly freed of its constriction, she rushed into nervous speech.

'Heavens, Mum, there's no need for that,' she protested. 'I can get a taxi . . .' she added wildly, only to receive a quelling look from Dominic.

'I'd be delighted to escort Christy to the ball,' he told her mother. 'In fact,' he looked up and across at Christy, holding her eyes and daring her to contradict him, as he said smoothly, 'I was going to ask her to come with me anyway.'

Liar, Christy thought bitterly, but there was no way she could say that to him with her parents looking fondly on at them as though . . .

She swallowed and gulped for air, her heart sinking as she saw quite plainly what her parents were thinking. Heavens, they had got her all paired off with Dominic! Her teeth dug into her bottom lip as she fought to stop herself from bursting into hysterical giggles. Later, when she was on her own with her mother, she would tell her that her matchmaking plans were doomed to failure—and why. It was on the tip of her tongue to ask Dominic acidly what he intended to tell Amanda, but she managed to resist the temptation. He might be taking *her* to the ball, but there was no doubt in Christy's mind whom he would be partnering once they were there.

'Put your dress on for me, I'm dying to see it.'

It was almost teatime, and Dominic had been gone for several hours. Christy and her mother were alone in the house, and dutifully Christy went into her own room and changed into her ballgown.

The look in her mother's eyes and the silence when she saw her brought a tiny thrill of pleasure to Christy's heart.

'Like it?' she teased.

'Oh, Christy, you look . . . fantastic . . .'

'There's a mask to go with it.' Christy demonstrated the white and silver disguise.

'It's lovely!'

Christy told her about how she had come by her outfit.

'What a wonderful idea! Is Meryl pleased about the baby?'

For the first time Christy was able to talk to her mother about Meryl and David's relationship without any constraint, knowing now that David was no longer attracted to her.

'Yes, I'm afraid there's always a penalty to be paid for marriage to that type of powerfully attractive man. Often, for all their intelligence, they can be like small children, fatally attracted to sticky but nutritionally useless sweets.'

Christy laughed at her mother's wry words.

'At least with your father I never had anything like that to worry about. Now Dominic's a very attractive and powerful man, but he has the strength and the resoluteness to avoid falling into that sort of trap. He doesn't have that sort of ego, for one thing, and for another, I suspect that he's a man who, once he loves, will stay faithful to that love through thick and thin.'

It was Christy's opening to warn her mother that she was cherishing misplaced hopes. Taking a deep breath, she said as lightly as she could, 'It sounds like

Amanda's going to be a very fortunate woman, then.'

In the silence that followed she couldn't bring herself to look at her mother, and then the latter said softly, 'Oh, my dear . . . I'm so sorry. Are you sure?'

'Yes,' Christy told her shakily. She forced a tight smile to her mouth as she turned to face her mother.

'I know how much you love him, Christy,' Sarah Marsden told her quietly, 'and I had thought . . . that is, your father and I . . .' she bit her lip. 'I'm more sorry than I can say, my dear. I thought this time . . . Now that you're both adults . . .'

Unable to bear listening to any more, Christy picked up the skirts of her dress and escaped into her own room. It was no use telling herself that it was stupid and, worse still, pointless for a grown woman of twenty-five to fling herself down on her bed and cry as though her heart was breaking for a man who would always be out of reach, but that was exactly what she did.

It was teatime before she had enough self-control to face the world again. Although she had bathed her face in cold water, her eyes remained suspiciously pink, but tactfully her mother said nothing about Dominic when she went back to ask her if she would like something to drink, instead chatting to Christy about her visit to London.

Two days later at a committee meeting of the fund-raising committee, Christy had a brief chance to speak to Dominic alone. The others had all left, and her father was standing outside the Vicarage talking to the Major.

'Dominic . . . about the Valentine's Night Ball.

There's really no need to pick me up and bring me back. I'd really prefer . . .'

'What? To be escorted by your married lover?' His mouth twisted with what was becoming familiar contempt. 'Why don't you ask him to do so, then, Christy, or are you afraid that he wouldn't leave his wife? Men like that rarely do, you know. The arrangement stands.'

Tense with frustration, Christy heard her father call out to her.

'You'd better go,' Dominic told her, opening the study door for her. She paused, torn between leaving and staying to argue with him, and then the phone rang.

As she hesitated he picked up the receiver, his voice deepening with pleasure, a smile curling his mouth as he said warmly into the mouthpiece, 'Amanda! Of course I've missed you . . .'

Later Christy wasn't quite sure how she got to the car. She only knew that she was shaking almost violently with a mixture of rage and jealousy as her father drove them home.

A phone call from the Major towards the end of the week to check up on the final details for the Valentine's Night Ball took Christy over to his Queen Anne house set against the backdrop of fields and hills. The house had once belonged to the Anthony estate, and the Major's father had purchased it from them just after the First World War.

He lived alone in the attractive red-brick mansion, looked after by a daily cleaning lady from the village, and by his batman, who had left the Army at the same time as the Major. Christy had only been inside the house once or twice, but she had heard a lot about it from her parents, who had been there to dinner and to play bridge on several occasions, and so she was already prepared for the almost spartan neatness when the Major's batman opened the door for her.

A long time ago, when he had first left the Army, the Major's pernickety ways had caused comment among the villagers, but now they were so used to him that he no longer drew their awe. Indulgent amusement was probably a closer description of the locals' attitude towards the Army-like way in which the Major ran his farm and his home, and Christy almost expected him to ask her if she was ready to take 'tiffin' as he escorted her into his book-lined study.

A painting of his father hung above the fire, and Christy noted their physical similarities as she sat down. The Major saw her studying the portrait and smiled at her.

'My father was a fine man,' he told her proudly, his smile turning to an almost brooding frown as he added, almost under his breath, 'even if there were those hereabouts who thought him beneath them . . .'

It was such an odd remark for him to make that Christy was nonplussed for a moment. As far as she was aware, everyone in the locale held the Major, if not in esteem, then in a certain amount of awe. He was known for his strict fairness and adherence to a code long since gone out of fashion, but a fairer or more moral man Christy doubted that anyone could find, and she had assumed that his family had been held in the same high repute.

However, she wasn't allowed to pursue the matter

even mentally, because the Major had a long list on his desk in front of him, and he was clearing his throat preparatory to getting down to business. It amused Christy to realise that he had even listed his queries alphabetically.

'Now, about the dancing.' He cleared his throat again, and if she hadn't known better Christy might almost have thought he was slightly embarrassed. 'I don't know what you have in mind, Christy . . . but I hope there'll be some music for the . . . er . . . older brigade to dance to.'

It took several seconds for his meaning to sink in, but once it had Christy hid a small grin. It wouldn't do to hurt his feelings by letting him think she was laughing at him.

'A great many of the tickets have been sold to people in their thirties and above,' she told him, 'and of course, since this is a romantic occasion, they'll be expecting appropriate dance music. I've provisionally booked a small combo who will play traditional waltz music, and of course the more romantic slower numbers. They come well recommended—they've played at a lot of local weddings—but if you'd like to interview them yourself . . . they've also offered to play for free since it's for a good cause . . .'

'No . . . no, that sounds excellent. Have you seen the ballroom at the Manor yet?'

Christy hadn't, and had been loath to ring up Lady Anthony and ask if she might lest it brought her into contact with Amanda. She had no idea whether or not the other woman had returned from London, although with the ball only just over a week away, it seemed unlikely that she would stay away much longer.

'Well, I've taken the liberty of arranging to show it to you today,' the Major suggested.

Christy wasn't quite quick enough to conceal her surprise. As far as she knew, the Major and Lady Anthony were such enemies that neither was likely to contact the other voluntarily.

'If you've got the time we could drive over there once we've gone through these queries.'

As David's personal assistant, Christy was skilled at ferreting out and finding the impossible; nevertheless she felt pleased when they reached the end of the the list and the Major complimented her on her work.

Everyone she had approached in connection with the ball had given their services freely. A local florist's had agreed to decorate the ballroom, and Christy liked the Major's suggestion that he contact an acquaintance of his who freelanced for *The Dalesman* and *Country Life* with a view to doing a piece on the ball for those publications.

Almost an hour later they set out for the Manor, Christy driving behind the Major in his ancient but immaculately kept Daimler. She was familiar with the grounds of the Manor from various fêtes and summer fairs, but she had only rarely been inside. Over the years the house had grown from the original Borders' fortress into a rambling collection of various styles of architecture, with the interior being remodelled by an eighteenth-century Anthony, who had happened to get on the right side of Elector George.

There was no sign of Lady Anthony when they were shown up an impressive flight of stairs to the ballroom.

The strong winter sunlight was not kind, revealing

unsightly patches of damp and cracks in the ornate plaster ceiling, and the Major shook his head sadly over the room's deterioration.

'I remember dancing here the year I was twenty-one. You should have seen it. I'll always remember the scent of the gardenias decorating the room. It was lit with chandeliers . . .' Lost in the past, he looked round the room.

Darkness and soft illuminations would be kind to its fading glory, Christy recognised, and nothing could ever detract from its elegant proportions. She felt a deep inward sadness as she realised how impossible it must be for someone like Lady Anthony to afford all the restoration work that was necessary. Houses like these simply ate up money, and the families who had built and cherished them could often no longer afford their maintenance.

'Ronnie was twenty-one that year as well. He died at the beginning of the war.'

'Ronnie?'

'Celia's . . .' he caught himself up, his ruddy complexion darkening slightly, as he amended, 'Lady Anthony's husband . . . Ronald Anthony. He was her cousin. He was killed in action at the beginning of the war.'

Christy told her mother about the sadly deteriorating state of the ballroom when she returned home, and about the Major's revelations about the Anthony family.

'Yes, I seem to remember someone once mentioning that Lady Anthony was widowed as a bride. Her husband was the only heir to the title, I believe. I've also heard it rumoured that the marriage was an arranged one. Her father was apparently a very proud man. Since he had no sons of his own to inherit, he decided that his daughter should marry her only male cousin to preserve the family line.'

'I wonder if she loved him,' Christy mused.

'I don't know. Tell me, what have you got planned for the food?'

Christy allowed herself to be diverted. 'Everyone's been wonderfully helpful. The WI are providing the buffet, which reminds me, Mrs Neilson asked me if she could use your raspberry soufflé receipe—and they're taking care of setting up the tables and chairs in a couple of rooms off the ballroom. The Major's donating some salmon.'

The Major owned and fished a small slice of salmon river in Scotland, and Mrs Marsden grinned as Christy told her this.

'His freezer is full of the stuff, or so Mrs Fiddler says, but he hates parting with it normally.'

They went on to discuss the floral decoration of the ballroom, and they were still deep in discussion when Christy's father returned from work.

The weekend brought a forecast snap of cold weather, lowering the temperature and freezing the countryside in an icy grip. One afternoon when Dominic was expected to visit her mother, they received a telephone call to say that he had been delayed because of a major road accident just outside Setondale.

'Dr Savage had gone to the hospital with the ambulances,' the receptionist told Christy. 'He may have to stay to help out in the operating theatre, but I'll be in touch with you as soon as I know anything.'

Christy's mother shivered slightly when Christy told her. 'Poor souls; I only hope that all of them are all right.'

'What I can't understand is why Dominic chose to come back here,' Christy mused, following her own private thoughts. 'He's so well qualified he could work anywhere . . .'

'Setondale is his home, Christy,' her mother told her gently. 'His father and his grandfather both practised here.'

'Well, I can't see Amanda settling down to live in Setondale.' She said it crossly, not wanting to admit even to herself how much she envied Lady Anthony's god-daughter. She was far too sensible to deceive herself that if Amanda hadn't been around, Dominic might have . . .

Might have what? Fallen in love with her? She grimaced slightly to herself. Sexually she might be able to arouse him, but emotionally Dominic felt nothing for her . . . nothing at all.

When the receptionist rang through later in the afternoon to say that Dominic would not be able to visit the house until the following day, Christy told herself that it was a good thing that she had an appointment with the florist that would take her out of the house. She didn't want to see Dominic.

So why the feeling of disappointment and pain gathering deep inside her?

Because she was too foolish to be able to stop herself from loving him and yearning after him like a stupid adolescent, Christy derided herself bitterly.

CHAPTER SEVEN

TWO DAYS before the ball they had snow. Christy was in a fever of panic when she woke up and saw the ominous colour of the sky, and the white blanket already lying inches deep outside.

'Don't worry,' her mother consoled her when she confided to her her dread that the ball would be poorly attended because of the weather. 'Folks around here are tough. They won't let a little thing like a snowfall put them off.'

Although she was normally a good patient, over the last few days her mother had been extremely restless. The locum who had called to see her in Dominic's stead had pronounced that this was a good sign which showed that she was recovering well, but he had still counselled plenty of rest and no excitement.

'It's not fair,' she grumbled lightly now. 'I'm missing out on all the fun.'

The 'fun' to her mother meant the organisation, Christy recognised, suppressing a small smile, inwardly sympathising with her parent even while outwardly she remained obdurate about allowing her to do anything.

Already a brainwave of her mother's earlier in the week had resulted in Christy haring off to Newcastle with her father to buy as many heart-shaped tins and moulds as she could get her hands on. Members of the WI had been exhorted to search through their cupboards for these receptacles, so that a variety of heart-shaped desserts could be provided in tune with the theme of the evening.

Lady Anthony had very generously made the enormous kitchens at the Manor available to those members of the local community who were responsible for preparing the buffet, and Christy knew that her mother positively ached to be down there among them.

The colour scheme for the evening was pink and silver against a background of white. An inspired and totally unexpected, not to say generous, gift of a hundred metallic silver heart-shaped balloons had arrived by post from Meryl earlier in the week—she had spotted them in one of the Knightsbridge gift shops, she had informed Christy over the telephone, and had promptly bought their entire stock.

Meryl sounded so happy and bubbling over with self-confidence that Christy felt it was safe to ask her how things were.

'Fantastic,' she had told her promptly. 'The news that he's to be a father once more has stunned David. He's thrilled, of course, but he insists on treating me like fragile crystal.'

'And you're complaining?'

'Not really. Which reminds me, when junior does arrive, I shall require you to be godmama.'

Luckily the snow stopped falling just before lunch.

'I'm supposed to be meeting the florist àt the Manor this afternoon,' Christy told her mother as they shared the soup she had made. 'I don't know whether to cancel it.'

'Just as long as you aren't contemplating driving

yourself there you should be all right. Why don't you give the florist's a ring, and if they're still keen to go, order a taxi.'

Christy took her mother's advice. The woman who owned and ran the local flower shop confirmed that she was prepared to drive out to the Manor, and as they arranged that morning Christy's father arrived home to sit with the invalid.

'Honestly, you don't need to do this now,' Sarah Marsden protested. 'Nothing's going to happen to me.'

'No, it isn't,' Christy agreed firmly, 'because we won't let it. Dad and I both know what would happen if we left you alone. You'd be out of bed and down in the kitchen in no time at all.'

Because the snow was fresh the taxi had no difficulty in getting through to the Manor. Christy got out and paid the driver, tensing as she saw Dominic's car draw up and park.

She had to wait for change, and she saw Dominic get out, his dark head bare, his hair ruffled by the chill breeze. He looked at her without smiling, his expression almost brooding in intensity. She longed to go up to him and touch him ... just touch him, nothing else. Who are you kidding? she asked herself bitterly; nothing but knowing that he loved her with the same direct intensity with which she loved him would ever be enough to satisfy the ache inside her.

'You look pale. Are you feeling all right?'

She hadn't seen him move, and she swung round, feeling vulnerable and shaky, her fear of revealing her vulnerability to him making her sound terse and remote.

'I'm fine.'

'You don't look it. It must be the strain of loving a man who is committed to someone else.'

She was too shocked to conceal her expression from him. Her face went white, her eyes enormous pools of agonised pain.

'Christy, I . . .' He spoke almost roughly, his own eyes darkening, his voice harsh as he demanded thickly, 'Is it really worth it? Why don't you give him up? Let his wife . . .'

She almost sagged with relief as she realised what he meant. For one dreadful moment there she had thought he had guessed . . . that he had known how she felt about him.

A small van was bumping down the lane towards them, and she pulled away, just as the front door of the Manor opened and Amanda came out.

She was wearing a silk dress that emphasised the slimness of her legs and the full curves of her breasts. Mentally comparing her elegant appearance with her own cord and jumper-clad body, Christy only just managed to suppress a faint sigh. No wonder Dominic was hurrying towards the other woman. She wondered if he realised yet that Amanda wanted more than the same sort of casual affair he had offered her. Or perhaps where Amanda was concerned he was prepared to offer more.

'Sorry if I'm late . . .'

Wrenching her attention away from the couple walking ahead of them into the house, Christy turned to greet the woman hurrying to join her.

The front door had been firmly closed behind Amanda and Dominic, and Christy wondered if

Amanda had simply not realised that they were there or was deliberately trying to be rude.

Lady Anthony herself showed them up to the ballroom, rather to Christy's surprise. She moved a little awkwardly, no doubt because of her arthritis, but it was still possible to see traces of the girl she must once have been.

Louise Fisher from the flower shop nodded her approval when she saw the room. She and Christy had already discussed what she intended to do, and Christy had shown her the balloons that Meryl had sent.

'You know, it's a real challenge to do something like this . . . And what a beautiful room.'

She went on to discuss how she intended to decorate it while Christy and Lady Anthony listened.

'The last ball held here was for my husband's twenty-first,' Lady Anthony told them. For a moment a sad expression haunted her eyes. 'He was killed at the beginning of the war.'

'Yes, so the Major told me,' Christy responded.

Almost instantly Lady Anthony withdrew into herself, her expression hardening. 'My father told him he was never to set foot in this house again.'

Christy and Louise exchanged surprised looks.

'Had he and your father had a quarrel, then, Lady Anthony?' Christy asked gently, not sure whether or not she would be rebuffed.

'In a way . . . However, you haven't come here to talk about the past.'

Taking her hint that the subject was not one she wanted to pursue, Christy stood to one side while Louise studied the room. They were just discussing the mass of banked plants and flowers Louise intended to place in front of the raised stage which would hold the small band when Amanda walked in, her arm tucked proprietorially through Dominic's.

'Ah, there you are, my dear. We were just discussing the flowers.'

Amanda managed to look both bored and supercilious at the same time. 'Mummy always uses Moyses Stevens. She says that no one else can possibly compare with them.'

Christy, who knew the top people's florist's quite well through David, who always used them to supply flowers for his parties, flushed a little uncomfortably at Amanda's lack of tact, but Louise seemed perfectly calm and at ease.

'Yes, they are good, aren't they,' she agreed pleasantly. 'I was lucky enough to go on one of their courses a couple of years ago, and I certainly learned a lot.'

Christy nearly cheered at the pleasant way that Louise had put the other woman in her place, especially when Louise didn't linger over her victory but instead went on quietly to explain to them all just what she had in mind.

'Fresh flowers are very expensive at this time of year, so I'm hoping to get away with plenty of greenery and only the minimal amount of flowers. Pink and white, of course, to tone in with everything else.'

There were several rather tarnished mirrors hanging on the wall, and Louise explained how she hoped to provide floral frames for them. Even Amanda looked reluctantly impressed.

It was going dark before Louise was finished.

Christy glanced at her watch and asked Lady Anthony if she could possibly use her phone to ring for a taxi.

'There's no need for that,' Dominic told her in a clipped, almost strained voice. 'I'll run you back.'

'Oh, but darling, I wanted you to stay for supper. It's your first evening off this week . . . and . . .'

'I'm sorry, Amanda, but I've promised to have dinner with the Major. He gets rather lonely, you know.'

Dominic seemed to be looking at Lady Anthony as he spoke, and an incredibly far-fetched and surely impossible suspicion suddenly crossed Christy's mind. Could the Major and Lady Anthony possibly have been romantically involved at one time?

It seemed impossible, and yet . . . Telling herself that she was letting her imagination get the better of her, Christy tried to refuse Dominic's offer of a lift, but he wouldn't let her.

A cold east wind was blowing when they got outside. Christy huddled deeper into her padded jacket. She hadn't worn her fur since that last occasion, but now she wished that she had put it on. It made no difference her knowing that Meryl had chosen it for her; Dominic's remarks still hurt.

'Get in.'

Dominic unlocked the door and opened it for her. The inside of his car smelled of leather and some indefinable masculine odour that her body recognised as being part of Dominic himself.

It was shaming how readily her body responded to such minimal stimulation, and if she hadn't known herself better she might almost have described her reaction as wanton. It was hard not to give in to the temptation to remember what it had felt like to be held in his arms, to be kissed . . .

She tensed as Dominic settled himself beside her and started the engine. As he backed the car round skilfully she looked through the side window.

They were half-way down the lane before he spoke, his terse, 'I haven't thanked you yet for all the hard work you've put in for this ball, Christy,' making her say equally curtly,

'There's nothing to thank me for; after all, I'm not doing it for you personally, am I?'

After that he made no further attempts to engage her in conversation, and she told herself that she was glad.

As he stopped the car for her to get out, she made one more attempt to dissuade him from driving her to the ball, but to her consternation, instead of agreeing with her that his giving her a lift wasn't necessary, he said savagely, 'Oh, for God's sake, Christy! What are you trying to do? Make everyone else as aware as I am how much you loathe me? You know quite well that your parents will worry about you if . . .'

'Oh, all right.' She slammed his car door childishly as she walked away from him, giving vent to her temper. He was right, of course: her parents would worry, and her father wouldn't understand her insistence on getting a taxi when Dominic had volunteered to take her.

'Come and let me have a look at you when you're ready.'

If she ever managed to get ready, Christy thought fatalistically. It seemed as though the phone hadn't stopped ringing all day long with one query or another. She wasn't even sure that she could summon the energy to go to the ball. No, it wasn't that that was making her so reluctant to get ready, she acknowledged. It was the knowledge that she would have to watch Dominic with Amanda . . . watch them dancing together . . . watch them . . .

Stop it . . . stop it . . . she urged herself, clenching her hands into fists. She was deliberately tormenting herself.

No more snow had fallen, and she had managed to get in to Setondale at lunchtime to have her hair done. Privately she wasn't sure what she thought of the wild mane of curls that the stylist had teased from her locks.

The stylist, a pretty young girl, had assured her that she looked absolutely fantastic, and the torrent of wild curls was certainly in keeping with her gown.

She daren't risk a shower in case it flattened her hair, but fortunately she had had the forethought to have one before going out, and as she stripped off her clothes she caught the faint, lingering traces of her scented body lotion. As she smoothed more of it into her skin she wondered why on earth she was bothering. Women scented their bodies for the enjoyment of their lovers. Her hands stilled, her nails digging into the smooth firmness of her thigh as she tried not to imagine what it would be like to have Dominic as her lover.

That last summer she had gone swimming with him one day and had been both shocked and fascinated by the male structure of his body. In her mind's eye she could recapture the memory of the dark shadowing of hair covering his chest and disappearing beneath the top of his swimming shorts. That had been just before she had realised the true nature of her feelings for him, and she could still recall the squirming embarrassment-cum-excitement curling through her body as he stripped off.

'What's the matter?' he had teased her, tugging her hair with gentle fingers.

The smell of the summer grass and the scent of his skin were impressed on her senses for all time, and she could still recall the heart-thumping, dizzying realisation of how she felt about him.

'Dominic.'

She wasn't even aware of saying his name. Tears filled her eyes and she shook them away, despising herself for being so vulnerable.

She put on clean underwear: brief satin panties and a matching suspender belt in a pretty soft cream that had been a Christmas present from her parents. She couldn't wear a bra under her dress. She avoided her reflection in the mirror as she slid on silk stockings, and then pulled on her old dressing-gown before starting on her make-up.

The gauche, uncertain girl she had been when she first went to London no longer existed, and she applied skilled touches of colour to her eyes and skin with the expertise she had learned during her years as David's assistant.

Downstairs the grandfather clock sounded the hour. Soon Dominic would be here. Christy shivered slightly as she stood up and checked her evening bag. She was ready. All she had to do was put on her dress.

She stepped into it, swearing mildly under her

breath as she fought with the mass of petticoats. It zipped up more easily than she remembered, but then her mother had already commented that she seemed to have lost weight.

The dress had been designed for a play where every historical detail had to be exact, but it still came as a shock to realise how much of the upper curves of her breasts the lace-trimmed neckline revealed. And surely her curves had never been quite as provocative and luscious as they appeared to be now? The fabric moulded and held her breasts into a rounded fullness that made her frown and chew a little on her bottom lip.

Ridiculously, when she tried on her mask and looked at herself in the mirror she felt slightly better about the neckline of the dress, as though somehow hiding behind her mask gave her some sort or protection from her own awareness of her body.

She held her breath slightly when she went in to show her mother, but she needn't have worried. She made no comment at all about her neckline, instead marvelling at the beauty of her gown. When Christy drew her attention to her exposed breasts, her mother laughed and said robustly, 'I suppose it is rather provocative, but only in the nicest possible way.'

Even so, Christy was glad of the velvet cloak that Meryl had suggested that she hire, and she was very careful to keep it carefully closed when she heard the sound of Dominic's car, and her father opening the door to him.

'I'd better go,' she told her mother. 'Dominic will want to be there early.'

'Yes. He told me that most of the committee are

sitting together on the same table.'

They were, but Christy wasn't sure whether Dominic intended to join them. She suspected that Amanda would have plans of her own for the evening which wouldn't include sharing Dominic with the rest of them.

From the top of the stairs she looked down yearningly at where Dominic stood chatting to her father, knowing that she was shielded from him and that he couldn't see how avidly and needingly she looked at him. He was wearing a dinner suit, and a giant fist seemed to close round her heart as she looked down at him, tanned and dark-haired, and completely at ease in his no doubt expensive evening suit. He wore it with a familiarity that said that he felt completely at home in its tailored smoothness.

Perhaps that was what she needed. Christy thought sadly: to be reminded of the vast gulf in experience that now lay between them. He wouldn't have lived the life of a monk while he was in America, she was sure of that. *He* wouldn't have held himself aloof from sexual experimentation because his heart and mind was full of *her* image.

She saw him glance at his watch, light bouncing off the thin gold strap, and she started to walk downstairs.

'Ah, there you are,' her father beamed at her. 'Aren't we going to get a preview of the outfit?' He turned to Dominic before she could speak. 'I remember her first grown-up party dress, don't you, Dominic? She couldn't wait to show it off to you.'

They all laughed, but her father was the only one whose laughter was natural. There was simply no way she could remove her cloak and twirl round for her father's inspection with Dominic standing there watching her, and so she shook her head and said in a voice made husky with tension, 'I'm sorry, Dad, we'll have to go. We can't be late . . .'

She could feel the tension emanating from Dominic as he escorted her to his car, but it wasn't until she was sitting beside him as he drove down the lane that he spoke to her.

'What's the matter?' he demanded harshly. 'Were you afraid that your father would recognise it as a dress bought by a man for his lover? Is that why you wouldn't show it to him?'

For a moment she was too shocked to speak. Did Dominic honestly think that? She remembered how he had looked at the box when they were on the train and opened her mouth to contradict him, but the words died unsaid. What was the point of saying anything? Let him think what he wanted. Surely it was easier to endure his contempt and animosity than to have to battle against his physical desire, especially when she was so aware of her own weakness and how very vulnerable she was to him?

Not that she had anything to fear from him in that regard any longer, and as she met the cold condemnation in his eyes she marvelled that they had ever gleamed hot and molten with desire for her. Looking at him now, it seemed almost an impossibility. But he had wanted her, he had told her so, and she had turned away from him, heartsick because it was only desire and not love.

They weren't the first to arrive. Several other cars were already parked in front of the house. Anticipating Dominic's intention of opening the car door for her, Christy beat him to it, feeling idiotically gauche as he stepped back from the car and watched with a grim humourless smile.

'You're very wise,' he told her under his breath. 'If I put my hands on you feeling the way I do tonight, I might be tempted to indulge myself in violence. You have that effect on me, didn't you know?' he asked her savagely as she made a small sound of protest.

'Then I suggest you go and look for Amanda,' Christy told him bitterly. 'She looks to me like a woman who knows how to handle a violent male. She might even like it.'

Aghast at her own jealousy, she half stumbled in the drive. Sickness churned through her stomach. She wasn't sure which of them she hated the most— Dominic, for getting beneath her guard, or herself for allowing him to do so.

'Bitch!' She heard him curse as he caught up with her and took her firmly by the arm. 'It doesn't suit you, you know, Christy,' he told her, swinging her round to face him. 'Is that what he's done to you: turned you from a sweet, innocent girl into . . .'

'A woman?' she threw at him, wrenching her arm free. The door opened and she hurried inside. Dominic was close behind her.

With an almost bitter sense of satisfaction she watched Amanda detach herself from her god-mother's side and hurry across to them, promptly annexing Dominic. Christy already knew which room had been put aside as the ladies' cloakroom, and she made her way there without giving Dominic and Amanda a second glance.

The wives of several other members of the

committee, plus some of her mother's friends from the WI, were already there, and Christy exchanged hellos and smiles with most of them before taking off her cloak. She had been carrying her mask on her arm, and she paused in front of one of the mirrors to put it on.

Behind her she heard someone say, 'My dear, that is the most magnificient costume. I do envy you, even though I don't have the figure to wear it any longer.' Turning round, Christy recognised one of her mother's friends. 'Where on earth did you get it?'

Smiling, she explained.

'Oh, well, that explains it. It really is stunning. Yes, I can see Shakespeare's Kate in that, quarrelling with Petruchio.'

'I'd better get to the ballroom, and check that the musicians have arrived,' Christy excused herself.

In the ballroom only the wall lights were illuminated, with low-wattage bulbs, and the soft pink glow they cast had a softening effect on the room. The wooden floor had been polished by volunteers from the WI before being chalked, and the musicians were already in place on the small raised stage. One of them raised his head and whistled appreciately as Christy hurried towards them, and Christy dipped him a mock curtsy, only to tense as she felt the heated pressure of eyes boring into the back of her neck.

She knew before she turned round who was looking at her. Dominic was standing with Amanda, who was chatting animatedly to her godmother, far too intent on her own conversation to be aware of her escort's slow and thorough scrutiny of Christy's white and

silver figure. It was a long time before he lifted his eyes
to her face, and Christy felt the whole room sway
around her as she read the savage contempt in their
depths. She wanted to cry out against it, and like
someone under a numbing spell she moved slowly as
though through water as she dragged her gaze away
and tried to resume her conversation with the
musicians.

'Ah, Christy. Everything seems to be under control.
The ladies from the WI have provided a first-class
buffet. Have you seen it yet?'

Thankfully Christy turned to the Major, accepting
his invitation to, as he put it, 'Inspect the troops'.

'You're not supposed to be able to recognise me
with this mask on,' she teased him mock-
reproachfully.

'Oh, I'd recognise that red hair of yours anywhere!'

All the women were to retain their masks until
twelve o'clock when their partners, who would
presumably be quite well aware who they were, could
demand their removal or payment of a forfeit. This
had been Lady Anthony's suggestion, and Christy had
thought it a good idea, in view of the romantic theme
of the evening.

Within an hour most of the guests had arrived, and
the ballroom floor was pleasantly crowded. Christy
watched the dancers from the sidelines, trying not to
notice how well Dominic and Amanda danced
together, and how close their bodies were.

She didn't know how much more of Dominic's
contempt she could take. She had never thought him a
particularly egotistical man, but she could only

presume that his savagery towards her now sprang
from the fact that in his eyes she had turned him down
as her lover in favour of David.

She told herself that the Dominic she had loved
would never have behaved so cruelly, but it made no
difference at all to the way she felt about him.

The Major asked her to dance and she got up to do
so, the skirts of her dress swaying gracefully as she
moved. She was aware that her dress had caused
something of a stir, but she took no pleasure in the
knowledge. That one contemptuous look Dominic had
given her had stripped her defences from her, and the
evening had become something merely to be endured.

The Major danced surprisingly well, his olde-worlde
courtesy balm to her soul after Dominic's biting
sarcasm, but even so, she was aware that she didn't
have all the Major's attention. She had seen him
glance more than once at where Lady Anthony was
sitting and on some impulse she was reluctant to
analyse she said quietly to him, 'Lady Anthony looks
rather lonely; why don't you go and ask her to dance?'

'I would, but I know she'd refuse me.' He gave a
rather humourless bark of laughter. 'And it wouldn't
be the first time.' A shadow crossed his face. 'There
was a time when I thought . . . but I was foolish. Her
father wanted to keep the title in the family, and she
married Ronnie. We were in the same regiment, you
know.'

And the Major had loved her, Christy suspected,
her heart aching for him. Just for a moment she had
seen behind his stern mask to the man, and as he
glanced across the room to Lady Anthony, Christy
realised that he still loved her.

The music stopped just as they swung level with Lady Anthony's table. 'You dance very well, my dear, and in that dress you are quite the belle of the ball . . .' The faded blue eyes grew lightly wistful.

Acting on impulse, Christy said softly, 'The Major was just telling me that he would love to ask you to dance, but that he was frightened that you would refuse him.' She didn't dare to look at her companion, but even without doing so she was aware of his growing anger, and prayed that she had not made a terrible mistake.

To her relief she saw that Lady Anthony was slightly flushed and rather disconcerted, but far from displeased.

'Oh well . . . well . . . I rarely dance these days. My arthritis, you know.'

'Nonsense,' Christy heard the Major saying gruffly. 'Why, I remember when you were the best dancer for fifty miles around, you were so light on your feet.'

Almost unable to believe her eyes, Christy watched the Major reach out and bring Lady Anthony gently to her feet, just as the musicians started to play a waltz. Lady Anthony was smiling at him, as shy as a young girl.

Just as Christy had mentally prophesied, there was no sign of Dominic making any attempt to join the rest of their table when it came to the time for supper. She could see him sitting half-way across the room with Amanda, and she had to fight down the hot, smouldering jealousy corroding through her body.

She didn't eat very much, and excused herself as soon as possible, going down to the ladies' cloakroom to check on her appearance. Her face looked too pale, and her hands trembled as she applied more blusher and fresh lipstick.

She didn't touch her hair, studying herself only briefly as she slipped her mask back on. It transformed her face, giving it an odd, fey quality that was hard to define. Behind it her eyes flashed and glowed, the light playing on the rounded smoothness of her breasts. She still felt uncomfortable with the neckline of her gown, but there was nothing she could do about it, and in reality her outfit was far less revealing than the gauzy creation being worn by Amanda.

She must have stayed in the cloakroom longer than she intended because when she got back people were just beginning to drift on to the dimly lit floor, and as she stood watching them she heard the compère saying, 'Come on, ladies and gentlemen, in five minutes it will be midnight. Gentlemen, remember that if your partner refuses to unmask for you, you can demand a forfeit . . .'

She had to get away from here, Christy realised stubbornly, trying to control the pain savaging her. She simply didn't have the strength to stand and watch Dominic dance past her, holding Amanda in his arms.

She turned to leave the room, and stiffened as she felt a constraining hand on her arm.

'Our dance, I believe,' a familiar voice grated in her ear, and she turned in stunned surprise to look directly into the darkness of Dominic's eyes.

He took full advantage of her momentary shock to steer her in the direction of the dance floor, his fingers biting deep into her skin as he refused to let her pull away.

'What are you talking about, Dominic?' she protested as he stopped and swung her round to face him, his arms closing round her. 'We had no arrangements to dance together.'

'Didn't we? I thought it was implicit in the mere fact that I brought you here. Look around you, Christy. I'll bet there aren't many women here now who aren't dancing with the man who brought them.'

What he said was unarguably true, but that didn't lessen her own sense of shock.

She struggled against his constraining arms, protesting, 'You should be dancing with Amanda, not me.'

Her struggles brought her into closer contact with his body, her breast swelling tightly against his dinner-jacketed chest as she fought for breath.

All around them couples were swaying together in sensual closeness. Dominic bent his head and she felt the faint rasp of his jaw against her skin just below her mask. As she caught the familiar scent of his cologne all the fight drained out of her and she felt her body go limp against his. Instantly his arm tightened.

'We've always moved well together, you and I, Christy,' he murmured in her ear. 'Remember when I taught you to dance?'

'I've danced with a lot of other men since then, Dominic.'

She winced beneath the harsh bite of his fingers into her waist, and wondered what on earth it was that drove her to challenge him in this way. Why couldn't she just accept what the gods were prepared to give her without wanting more?

Her full skirts padded the sensation of Dominic's body moving against her own, but she was still aware of it, aware of him, and aware of the fact that beneath her stiffened bodice her breasts felt swollen and tender. Tears clogged her throat, and when the music stopped and Dominic made to remove her mask she checked him instinctively, not wanting him to see her weakness.

Too late she realised her mistake, as she heard him murmur sardonically, 'No? People are watching us, Christy, so I'll just have to take the forfeit instead.'

Lost in her own misery, she hadn't realised why Dominic had been attempting to remove her mask, and now, with several amused dancers watching them, it wasn't possible for her to protest that it was all a mistake. Even the compère had seen them, and around them people laughed as he called out, 'Well now, it seems as if we have at least one reluctant maiden in our midst. Tell me, sir, what do you intend to claim as your forfeit?'

Dominic seemed totally unfazed by all the amused attention and simply gave their audience a wholly deceptive and, to Christy at least, heart-stopping smile as he drawled laconically, 'What do you think?' And then he was tipping her head back against his arm and kissing her in full view of their delighted audience. Christy thought she had never been so embarrassed in her life, but she sensed that to say or do anything as the musicians struck up the opening bars of a deliberately provocative love song could only make matters worse.

Amanda was the first one to reach them as they left the dance floor, her eyes spitting venom at Christy as she slid her arm through Dominic's. She was wise enough to say nothing there and then, but Christy had no doubt that the other woman was far from pleased, for all the teasingly pouting looks she gave Dominic.

Christy excused herself, saying that she had promised to help the WI ladies clear away after supper, although in point of fact all she really wanted to do was to escape from the amused and, it seemed to her in her highly sensitive state, very knowing eyes that observed her hurried progress from the dance floor into the supper room.

After that she kept well away from the ballroom, parrying all the teasing remarks that came her way.

'My goodness, it was almost as good as watching *Gone With The Wind*,' one plump matron teased her, eyeing Christy with the sort of speculation that made her heart sink. She had little doubt that in no time at all she and Dominic would be the talk of the village, and how long would it be after that before people started remembering her old teenage crush on him—if they had ever forgotten it?

She was carrying plates out to someone's car when she realised how cold it had gone. The sky was brilliantly starry, the air so crisply fresh that it almost hurt to drag it into her lungs.

'We'll have more snow soon, you mark my words,' somone commented lugubriously. 'I can smell it in the air.'

So could she, Christy acknowledged, shivering as she hurried back inside.

People were starting to leave, and she would have given anything to avoid accepting Dominic's lift home, but it was too late now to order a taxi.

She went reluctantly to the ballroom, surprised but pleased to see that Lady Anthony and the Major were sitting together, apparently deep in conversation. The Major smiled at her as she walked past. 'Excellent affair, my dear.'

'Yes, it quite took me back to my girlhood,' Lady Anthony agreed.

Several other members of the committee added their praise as they started to drift away, and although Christy searched the ballroom twice, there was no sign of Dominic.

Fear and something else clutched at her heart. Perhaps she would have to organise that taxi after all, or beg a lift from someone else.

There was no sign of Amanda anywhere either, she noticed jealously.

She was just beginning to think she genuinely *would* have to make her way home alone when Dominic walked into the ballroom.

Amanda wasn't with him, but Christy could see quite distinctly the smudge of dark red lipstick staining his mouth. *Amanda's lipstick.*

Her whole body seemed to seize in one vast, agonising surge of pain so intense that it rooted her to the spot, unable to drag her eyes away from Dominic's face and that tell-tale scarlet brand.

'I think it's time we made a move.'

'I'll go and get my coat and meet you downstairs.'

She moved away from him like an automaton, passing Amanda on the stairs. Triumph gleamed febrilely in the older woman's eyes, and Christy knew that that smear of lipstick was both a deliberate declaration and a warning.

There was no doubt that Amanda wanted her to know that she considered Dominic to be her property. Well, she was welcome to him, Christy told herself bitterly; more than welcome.

CHAPTER EIGHT

'DOMINIC, what are you doing? You've just driven straight past my parents' gate,' Christy protested sharply, sitting up straighter in her seat.

'They won't be expecting you yet. I thought you might like a nightcap.'

She was too bereft of words to speak, simply staring at him as he skilfully turned the car into the drive of his own home.

That he should have brought her here instead of taking her straight home was the last thing she had expected. In fact, she had half imagined that once he had delivered her home safely he would drive back to the Manor and Amanda's undoubtedly welcoming arms.

'Don't be ridiculous,' she told him crossly. 'I don't want another drink. In fact, I don't want anything at all from you.'

'You don't?' His face was in the shadows as he leaned forward to silence the engine. 'That wasn't the impression I got earlier tonight,' he told her cruelly. 'However, I haven't brought you back here to make love to you, if that was what you were implying, Christy,' he added derisively.

'I didn't think you had,' she retaliated instantly. 'After all, you've got Amanda for that, haven't you?'

There was a moment's tense silence and then he was opening his door and sliding his lean length out.

'Let's get inside before we both freeze.'

She wanted to refuse, but the implacably determined expression on his face as he waited for her to join him warned her not to.

The icy wind seemed to bite right through to her skin, and she was shivering by the time she stood in the large hall.

It felt cold and slightly damp, and as though aware of her thoughts, Dominic said quietly, 'I intend to have central heating installed in the spring. Come on, we'll go into my study; it's warmer in there.'

Christy stood to one side as he knelt by the dying embers of the fire and threw on some fresh logs. A shower of sparks raced up the chimney, the scent of apple logs filling the room.

He hadn't bothered to switch on any lights, and the dancing flames licking round the logs cast mellow shadows over the shelves of books. A pair of thick velvet curtains had been drawn against the night, and Christy fingered the fabric absently.

'This is rather a large house for a single man . . .' Her skin flushed hotly as she realised that she had spoken her thoughts out loud. Dominic threw another log on the fire and dusted off his hands before standing up.

'It affords me a welcome degree of privacy, and it's convenient for almost everywhere in the practice. I had to find somewhere in a hurry, and it was either this, or a Victorian terrace in Setondale.'

So he hadn't bought the house with marriage and a family in mind. 'Amanda thinks it's got good potential,' he added casually, tossing the words at her over his shoulders as he moved towards one of the cupboards and removed a decanter and two glasses.

Christy watched him pour the ruby liquid through a red haze of jealousy. It bit into her with flames that burned hotter than those devouring the apple logs, scorching her like corrosive acid. She could barely see through the rage of jealousy and hurt roaring through her body, and her wayward tongue raced into hasty speech before she could silence it, her voice unnaturally high and hurried as she cried bitterly, 'Does she now? I'd be very surprised if she agreed to settle up here, though, Dominic. I realise that she wants you very badly, but I should have thought Harley Street was more what she has in mind than Setondale.'

Like someone caught up in a nightmare, she froze as she watched Dominic tense and then put down the decanter. Prisms of light from the fire glittered off the crystal, and she was amazed that her brain could take note of such trivia when it also knew the enormity of what she had just said.

There was no kindness in the way he smiled at her as he turned to face her, and it seemed to Christy in her fear that there was an almost demonic quality to the way his skin seemed stretched tight over his facial bones.

'Well, now,' he said softly, 'that's a revealing statement if ever I heard one. You wouldn't be jealous of her, by any chance, would you?'

Appalled by what her unruly tongue had trapped her in, Christy blazed furiously, 'What could I be jealous of? The fact that she goes to bed with you? I was the one who turned down that opportunity—remember?'

He was across the room in half a dozen strides,

gripping her arms in a hurtful furious strength.

'My God, you just *don't* know when to stop, do you?'
he breathed thickly.

She struggled against him, fear and desire mingling
in almost equal quantities, but her struggles seemed
only to incite the fires she could see blazing in the
depths of his eyes.

'Stop it, Christy!' He shook her almost as though
she weighed no more than a rag doll, and in an agony
of bitterness, she raised her hand to claw desperately
at his face. He jerked his head out of the way just in
time, and then Christy heard him swear and saw the
dark fury in his face.

It was too late to protest or plead for mercy, and
time seemed to stand still in a preternatural silence as
he slowly lowered his head towards her. She could
hear the fiery crackle of the logs, and the agonised
sound of her own breathing. A tortured moan was
smothered in her throat as she felt the savagely harsh
pressure of his mouth against her own.

There was nothing sensual or arousing about the
way he kissed her; he was punishing her, deriding her,
but in spite of everything she could feel the sudden
upsurge of passion flooding through her, as though her
body had starved so long for his touch that it was ready
even to respond to this . . . this parody of passionate
need.

She could feel the edge of his teeth against her
mouth, and felt herself shiver in physical response as
he used them without compunction to part the swollen
softness of her lips. When his tongue thrust possessively into her mouth, she felt the molten heat slide
through her veins.

Against her body she could feel the rapid, uneven thud of Dominic's heart. Somehow her arms had locked round his neck, holding him against her. His tongue touched her lips, tracing their swollen curves. She felt the shiver that ran through him, hardly recognising the husky, raw note of pain in his voice as he muttered against her mouth, 'God, Christy . . . what is it you do to me?'

His mouth touched hers again, gently this time as though he wanted to caress away her pain. She could easily have pulled away from him, but she didn't, abandoning herself instead to the heady tide of pleasure that swept her away from reality as his mouth lingered on hers.

'Christy . . .'

She shivered responsively to the note of need deepening the way he said her name. She could feel the heat of his hands where they held her, and beneath the bodice of her gown her breasts ached to be caressed.

His mouth was no longer punishing as it moved on hers, all anger and contempt expunged by the need that seemed to engulf them both. Without him saying it she could sense his desire, feel it in the way his hands stroked over her back, moulding her against him. She clung to him in the firelight, giving herself up completely into fate's hands, wanting him too much to fight any longer.

'Christy, you've no idea what you do to me. I've wanted you for so long.'

The muttered words shivered across her skin, her head falling back against his shoulder as his mouth explored the soft column of her throat. Tiny spears of delight shafted through her, her body so responsive to his touch that he made a sound of muttered frustration against her skin.

'Let me make love to you, Christy. Let me show you how much I want you.' His hands reached for the fastenings at the back of her dress, his body tensing as she stepped gently away from him.

She couldn't stop herself from blushing softly as she saw him looking at her. A dark flush of passion stained his cheekbones, his eyes feverishly alight as he reached for her.

'Let me unfasten it,' she said softly. 'The catches . . .'

She had stepped into a pool of light cast by the fire, and suddenly his expression darkened. Fear, and remembrance of that earlier rejection, held her immobile, her lips trembling as she asked huskily, 'What is it, Dominic, what's wrong?'

'It's that damned dress . . .'

She stared at him, ridiculously hurt. 'What's wrong with it?'

'*He* bought it for you,' Dominic told her savagely. 'That's what's wrong with it.' He moved towards her, his face contorting paganly as he reached for the front of her gown, and with one savage wrench ripped the bodice open.

Too shocked to correct him Christy could only stare down at the destruction he had wrought.

'Dominic!'

'Take it off, for God's sake,' he demanded thickly. 'I can't bear seeing you in it, Christy . . . I can't bear knowing . . .' He made a raw, thick sound in his throat and reached for her again, dragging the expensive fabric away from her body, until it fell in a pool at her feet.

For what seemed like a long time she was too stunned to move. The firelight played softly on the creamy contours of her breasts, but she was barely aware of the look in Dominic's eyes as his gaze absorbed their rounded perfection crowned with the pouting provocation of her erect nipples.

'Christy . . . My God . . . you're so beautiful. More beautiful than I could ever have imagined.' He moved to her then, lifting her away from the desecration of her gown. 'To think I once refused all this.' He closed his eyes and she saw him swallow painfully, that tiny vulnerable movement in his throat cutting through her shock.

'Do you still hate me for that?' His fingers seemed to shake slightly as they caressed her throat and moved up to tilt her face so that she was forced to look at him.

Hate him? She stared into the brilliance of his eyes, and moistened her dry lips with the tip of her tongue. His eyes followed the movement intently, heat shooting through her as he pulled her hard against him and she felt the surge of his desire against her body. His hands slid down to her hips, urging her closer to him. His eyes closed so that his dark lashes lay vulnerably against the tautness of his skin as he bent his head and kissed her with a fierce and totally overwhelming passion.

She had no thought of holding back, of even trying to stop him. Her body surrendered eagerly to his touch, her breasts crushed against his chest.

He released her briefly to tug off his jacket. Beneath the fine cotton of his shirt she could see the heavy play of muscles and the dark shadowing of hair, and her fingers itched to unfasten his shirt. Lost in her own private daydreams, she suddenly realised how tense he was.

A soft flush of colour spread over her body as she saw the way he was looking at her.

'My God, you can't know how much I've wanted this.'

His hands touched her, sliding softly up over her ribs to cup her breasts. Fierce surges of delight rocketed through her, her breasts swelling wantonly against his palms. She shuddered in molten desire beneath the arousing movement of his thumbs against her nipples.

'You like that?'

His voice was unfamiliar, raw and husky with male desire, and she thrilled to the sound of it.

'Dear heaven, I nearly went mad with the need to do this years ago . . . do you know that?'

She quivered in response, making no demur when he picked her up and carried her across to the settee, sitting down on it, holding her in his arms.

Firelight played across the planes of his face and she raised almost timid fingers to caress it. Shocking waves of delight shuddered through her as he held her palm to his mouth, slowly caressing it. She could feel her breasts peaking in wanton delight.

'Christy, I want you so much. Touch me . . . undress me . . .'

Which of them was it who was shaking as he transferred her hand to the front of his shirt, helping her to unfasten that first button? Beneath her fingertips his skin felt moist and burning hot. She felt him shudder finely as she slid her hand against his skin, stroking through the soft thickness of his body hair. He groaned deep in his throat, and with great daring she did what she had wanted to do from the first moment she had witnessed that small betraying gesture: she placed her mouth against the maleness of his throat and caressed it with the tip of her tongue.

His response to her went far beyond her wildest fantasies; never had she dared even once to imagine him going wild in her arms like this, responding to her, showing her how much he liked what she was doing.

The collar of his shirt impeded her progress down towards his shoulder and she unfastened the rest of the buttons, tugging the fabric away from him and pushing it off his skin.

She felt his fingers curl into her hair as she slowly caressed his body, taking her time as she savoured every inch of warm male flesh. Her fingertips stroked lightly along the line of body hair that disappeared beneath the waistband of his suit, registering the taut firmness of his belly as her hand lingered possessively there.

She wanted to feel all of him against her without the barriers of any clothes, but shyness overwhelmed her. She had no experience in undressing men, and she was frightened of destroying the delicate spell they had woven around themselves with clumsy inexperience, so she simply let her hand lie flat against him as her mouth traced the hard muscles of his chest, and her tongue stroked tentatively against the pebble hardness of one flat male nipple.

She felt him move, pushing himself against her, his hands sliding to her hips and then down to her thighs before moving up again to slide under the edge of her satin briefs to cup the rounded softness of her bottom and pull her against him.

The tension invading her lower body was awesome and familiar. She had desired him like this before, but never with such immediate intensity. Logic and reason were totally suspended, only instinct prevailing.

'I've got to feel you against me ... all of you.' Dominic muttered, releasing her and standing up.

She couldn't look at him, but she heard the metallic sound of his zip, and the slither of cloth against flesh.

He came to her from the shadows of the fire, tautly male and the embodiment of all her feminine fantasies. Dark shadows concealed much of his body from her as he kneeled on the floor at her feet, cupping her instep in one hand while the other dealt with the fastenings of her stockings.

She could almost see his tension at her body's unmistakable response to his touch, the look glittering darkly in his eyes as he raised them to her face, making her fear momentarily that he meant to tear what was left of her clothes from her and lay her bare to his gaze, but instead he undressed her slowly and painstakingly, his fingers a tormenting caress against the insides of her thighs as he slid down her stockings.

Her heart seemed to stand still in her breast as he lifted her to tug down her briefs, and she felt the heat of his breath against her skin.

At last, when they were both naked, he simply kneeled and stared at her until she was quivering with a mixture of self-consciousness and need. His hand reached out and caressed the curve of her throat and then slid down to her shoulder.

'Just perfect,' he murmured softly. 'Perfect.'

And then, still kneeling before her, he took her in his arms and kissed her as she had dreamed of him kissing her, his mouth both tender and demanding; hungry for her and yet feeding her own need.

'I want you so much. You have no idea.' His mouth slid moistly over her throat, and caressed the fragile bones of her shoulder. His hands had found her breasts and were slowly caressing them. His mouth moved slowly, oh so slowly over her skin, until she was ready to cry out with need, and then she felt its warmth against the curve of her breast and she closed her eyes in a sudden agony of desire, digging her nails into his shoulder as she sought desperately for something to cling on to in the fierce maelstrom of delight that had seized her.

His tongue touched her nipple, gently circling the deep pink flesh before delicately brushing over it, making her cry out in shocked delight.

'I could almost believe that no one has ever touched you like this before.'

Dominic's voice was dazed, drugged almost, and she clung to the aroused desirous sound of it rather than listening to the words. It seemed impossible to believe that he could not know how she felt about him, and that he was not just the first, but the only one.

'Do you like that, Christy?' His voice had a slurred, almost drunken quality to it now as his tongue caressed her nipple a little more roughly.

'And this, do you like this?' The words were almost lost as he pressed his open mouth against her aching flesh and then sucked fiercely on it. Spasms of pleasure arced through her, bringing soft cries of delight to her lips as she pushed herself eagerly against the hot demand of his mouth, abandoning herself to the sensuality of her own nature.

Over and over again Dominic caressed the aching peaks of her breasts until she was shivering with a surfeit of pleasure.

'I should take you upstairs to bed,' he told her hoarsely as he lifted her down to lie beside him in front of the fire, 'but I can't wait that long for you.'

She was the one in shadow now, while the firelight revealed the taut impatience of his body to her. She shivered, her eyes and hands drawn to the male perfection of his body, wanting to touch him, but almost afraid to do so.

'God, yes, Christy . . . yes,' he groaned against her mouth, seeing the desire in her eyes and taking her hand to place it against his body.

Beneath her fingers she could feel the fierce throb of male desire, and she gave herself up to letting him show her how he liked her to touch him.

'I can't stand much more of this. I want you too badly.' His voice sounded hoarse and thick as though it had difficulty in escaping from his taut throat.

Her body welcomed the heavy weight of his as he moved her so that he could lie between her thighs. Her pulses hammered against her skin. She wanted him so much. She moved her hips, writhing impatiently against him, and heard him catch his breath. His hands moved over her body touching her . . . even in his extremity of need making sure that she really was ready for him, Christy recognised intuitively.

No one had ever touched her so intimately, but her

body felt no shyness or self-conscious hesitancy, impatient for more than the delicate caress of his fingers against her eager flesh.

'Dominic.' She moaned his name, without being aware that she had done so, and felt him surge against her.

'Yes,' he said fiercely against her mouth. 'Yes.'

And he moved and she felt the awesome matching of their bodies; hers untutored but eager to accommodate and welcome the powerful thrust of his, his knowledgeable but held in check by a mind that cared enough about her sex to want to give as well as take pleasure.

All these things Christy dimly recognised somewhere beneath the flood of desire swelling inside her, just as she also recognised and registered the instinctive tightening of muscles unused to such intimate pressure.

Immediately her body registered Dominic's faint hesitation, but reality had long ago been left behind and her hips lifted and moved, enticing him, her legs wrapping round him, holding him within her, so that he was forced to respond and carry her with him though the sharply searing pain that faded as quickly as it had started and upwards to a place far beyond any mortal boundaries where they could both share the explosive delight that ran like quicksilver through their bodies, contorting them in delirious spasms of pleasure that went on and on into infinity before finally leaving them both exhausted and spent.

From a great distance away Christy heard Dominic call her name. She could feel tears of happiness gathering in her eyes as she opened them to look at him.

'For God's sake, it's too late for tears now,' she heard him saying roughly, but already the world was slipping away from her and she was sliding into a deep, warm, black abyss.

She came round almost immediately to find that Dominic had propped her up against some cushions he had taken from the settee and covered her with his shirt.

She could smell the scent of him on it and she wanted to curl into it and wrap it round her, but he was standing in front of her, zipping up his trousers, frowning down at her.

'Christy, for goodness' sake, why didn't you tell me you were a virgin?' She heard the censure in his voice and recoiled from it, watching his mouth tighten.

'Oh, God ... don't be even more stupid than you already have. Why, if you wanted a man that badly ...'

It was as though he had driven a sword straight through her heart.

'You were the one who made the first move,' she reminded him shakily. She felt at a disadvantage lying here at his feet covered in nothing more than a cotton shirt. 'Please pass me my clothes.'

He obeyed her, almost throwing them at her. The front of her dress was ripped almost to the waist. How on earth was she going to explain that to the hirers?

'I'm sorry about your gown.'

He sounded more indifferent than sorry, and self-defence made her snap at him,

'You were wrong you know—David didn't buy it for me. I hired it.'

'Then, of course, I'll pay for the damage.'

She couldn't believe that not ten minutes ago they had been sharing the ultimate human experience. It was like stepping into a surrealistic nightmare.

'I shouldn't have made love to you like that,' he said grittily. 'I had no right. If I'd known that you were a virgin . . .'

Of course he wouldn't have made love to her if he'd known, Christy acknowledged. He had expected her to be as experienced as he was himself; he had desired her and had felt free to want a woman who had other lovers, in a way he had not felt free to want her seventeen-year-old self. Sickeningly, she wondered if he thought she would expect some sort of commitment from him now, and if he was trying to warn her off. The humiliation of it struck right through to her aching soul.

'It does take two, Dominic,' she told him brittlely. 'I shouldn't have let you. You'll have to put it down to my frustration at losing David . . .'

'Losing him?'

'Yes, he and Meryl have gone to live in the States.'

'You mean you bargained for him with your virginity and now that he hasn't taken the bait, you decided you might as well get over your physical frustration with me, as well as with anyone else.'

It sickened her that he could think such a thing of her, but it offered her an escape route with her pride intact, so she acknowledged his words with a brief inclination of her head.

'We were both using one another, weren't we?' she

suggested with a tight smile. 'I suspect that I was no more than a substitute for Amanda.'

'Amanda's looking for marriage ... a second husband. I can't give her those things.'

He sounded almost abstracted, as though Amanda's wants were of very little importance to him, but Christy knew better. Sick at heart, she turned away from him.

'I think I'd better go ...'

He seemed reluctant to move.

'You ... I ...' He frowned and turned to look at her. 'If I hurt you in any way ...'

Christy knew what he meant and her face burned. He was, after all, a doctor, but she still felt humiliated that he could revert to a professionalism so soon after arousing her to heights that still lingered inside her.

'I'm fine,' she told him shortly. 'I want to go home, Dominic.'

'I'll take you.'

It was something of a shock to discover that she had been with him for a little more than an hour. The outside light burned over her parents' front door, but there was no sound from their bedroom as she tiptoed past. That was just as well; it would have been very difficult to find an excuse for her ruined dress. When she had taken it off she packed it away carefully in its box, so that no one else could see it.

Her body ached slightly now, but it was a pleasurable, voluptuous ache, an ache in fact, that reminded her body of the pleasures it had known and that held out the lure of repeating them.

Only in her case there would be no repetition; she

knew that. Dominic had simply used her, but she couldn't wholly blame him; after all, she had made no attempt to stop him, had she? Indeed, some people might say that she had actively encouraged him.

CHAPTER NINE

SOMEHOW life went on, although to Christy, in a daze of misery and pain, it seemed to have become something to be endured rather than enjoyed.

Her mother was now spending several hours a day out of bed, and Christy was at great pains to be unavailable whenever Dominic called at the house.

The shock of his arrival the day after the Valentine Ball still lingered with her. She had expected that he would be as eager to avoid her as she was him. She had told him then, without giving him the chance to speak to her, that she didn't want to see him again. She couldn't have borne him guessing how she felt about him and pitying her for it.

Luckily the hire company had been able to get the dress repaired, and now, if she was sensible, she would put the entire events of that night right out of her mind.

The only trouble was that no matter how firm she was with herself during the daytime, at night in her dreams she lost complete control, and dreamed of Dominic again and again, often waking up with tears still damp on her skin. Only this morning her mother had remarked on her wan expression and loss of weight, commenting that anyone would think that she was the one who had been ill.

Soon her mother would be able to manage without

her. Originally Christy had contemplated staying in
Setondale and finding a job in either Newcastle or
Alnwick, but that had been before she had realised
that Dominic had come home.

She knew that her parents were perturbed and
concerned by the abrupt change in her, but although
once or twice her mother had tried to bring the
conversation round to Dominic, Christy had fobbed
her off. The way she felt about him was far too painful
to discuss with anyone else.

Perhaps if Meryl had not been away in Los Angeles,
she might have been able to talk to her. Only this
morning Christy had received a letter from her
confirming the date of the baby's expected birth, and
telling Christy that David had still had no success in
replacing her. It was too late now to acknowledge that
she would have been wiser to have gone with them.
She had made her decision with the best intentions.

The end of the month brought fresh snowfalls, and
the knowledge that their lovemaking was not going to
result in a child. While logically she knew she ought to
be relieved, and that she had been a fool to take such a
risk, deep down inside Christy was aware of an
atavistic sense of loss and failure, as though somehow
in not conceiving the child of the man she loved she
had shown herself to be less of a woman.

She reasoned with herself that an illegitimate child
was the very last thing she wanted, but even while she
knew it to be true, there was still a feeling of emptiness
inside her.

'Dominic was asking after you yesterday,' her
mother commented, watching her as she stood

motionless before the sitting-room window staring out at the white landscape. Blizzard conditions had been forecast for later in the day, but as yet there was no sign of it in the clear deep blue arc of the sky and the brilliant glitter of the sun. Despite the sunshine, it was bitterly cold, well below freezing, and only that morning had the snow-plough cleared the way up the lane.

'Christy, can't you tell me what's wrong? Can't I help at all?' her mother asked sadly when Christy made no response to her earlier remark. 'You can't go on like this. You're losing weight . . . you've become so withdrawn that your father and I hardly recognise our daughter any more, and Dominic doesn't look much better. If you've quarrelled, surely you could make it up?'

'It wasn't that sort of quarrel,' Christy told her heavily, refusing to turn round. The very sound of Dominic's name on someone else's lips was enough to start the silly weak tears she cried at night in the privacy of her room flowing again.

'Your father tells me that Amanda has gone back to London.'

The sensation that jolted through her, hope mingled with despair, warned her how very vulnerable she was. She told herself that Amanda's departure meant nothing, and that in any case, even if Dominic's relationship with the other woman had petered out, there was still absolutely no hope of him every feeling about her the way she did about him.

By his very words to her about Amanda's desire for a second marriage, he had shown how far any sort of permanent commitment was from his own mind, and she loved him far too much to be his partner in a meaningless sexual affair.

'Talking of Amanda, I've heard another fascinating piece of gossip about the Andrews family. You'll never guess what. The Major and Lady Anthony are going to get married! Apparently he's been in love with her for years, and they had planned to get married but her father refused his permission. He insisted that Lady Anthony marry her cousin, and she and the Major quarrelled bitterly about it. The Vicar's wife told me the whole story. The ceremony is to take place in the Manor's private chapel, and there's to be a wedding breakfast there afterwards. I think it's one of the most romantic things I've ever heard of, don't you? I suppose he's never stopped loving her for all this time.'

It was romantic, and Christy was pleased for them both, but somehow hearing about the happiness of others only served to emphasise her own misery.

'I hope the snow holds off,' she heard her mother sigh. 'Your father and I are due to visit the Hopkinses tomorrow. We haven't seen them since before Christmas.'

Helen and Bill Hopkins were very close friends of Christy's parents and lived in Alnwick. They had spent Christmas and New Year with their daughter and her family in Leeds, but had recently returned, and apparently Dominic had agreed that her mother was now well enough to go and visit them.

'I know Helen would be delighted to see you if you want to come with us.'

Christy shook her head. 'No, thanks, Mum, I'm not

feeling very sociable at the moment. In fact, now that you're properly on the road to recovery, I shall have to do something about finding myself another job. I'll have to start getting the London papers.'

'Oh, but Christy, your father and I had hoped . . . Oh well, it's your life, my dear.'

Early the next morning Christy's parents set out for Alnwick. They had been gone less than an hour when the sky clouded over ominously, the wind picking up in velocity. Watching the first furious flurries of snow drifting in the high-speed winds, Christy shivered, and prayed that her parents made it to their friends safely.

Half an hour later when the phone rang and she heard her father's voice she was not surprised when he told her that they had decided to stay over in Alnwick and spend the night with their friends.

'I think you're very wise, Dad. It's snowing so heavily I can barely see the drive from the window, and it's drifting like mad.'

'Yes, it's the same here, although it's only just started. You must have got it before us. The local forecast isn't at all good, and the last thing your mother needs right now is to be stranded in a snowdrift. She's worried about you, though, Christy. Will you be all right on your own?'

'I'm a big girl now, Dad. I've been living on my own for several years—remember?'

She heard her father chuckle and was glad that she had managed to reassure him. She felt guilty because she knew that her parents had been worried about her.

She knew that she ought to make an effort to seem more cheerful. After another five minutes on the phone she managed to reassure her mother that she wasn't either going to starve or freeze to death in the brief space of twenty-four hours, and then she hung up.

The day stretched endlessly in front of her. It was only just lunchtime, although outside it was almost dusk, and it was snowing so heavily it was impossible to see where earth ended and sky began. She hadn't exaggerated when she told her father that it was impossible to see the lane from the window, and when she went to open the back door to bring in a supply of logs from the outhouse, just in case the central heating should happen to go off, the force of the wind whipped it from her fingers, smashing it back against the wall with a harsh thud.

Already snow had drifted over a foot deep against the door, and she had to go back inside and don her anorak and wellies before she could go and get the logs.

It took her several journeys to bring in enough. Her father, with almost a lifetime's experience of winter blizzards, had advised her to keep the sitting-room fire going at all times, and even to sleep down there if necessary should the central heating fail.

She was just stamping the snow off her wellingtons when she heard the sound of a car engine. Disbelievingly she stared towards the lane, watching the blue-grey shape of a Land Rover emerging through the blizzard. It stopped opposite the gate, the engine left running as its driver got out.

Even clad in wellies and a thick padded jacket, Christy recognised Dominic. His dark head was bare, his hair whipped by the wind and whitened by flakes of snow.

What was he doing here?

He didn't speak until he drew level with her, his curt, 'Christy, I need your help,' making her stare silently at him.

'Look, I haven't got much time. One of my patients has gone into premature labour. She lives in one of the hill farms, and there's no way we're going to be able to get her into hospital in time. Luckily they'd got this Land Rover in for a service in the garage in Setondale, and as it was an emergency they lent it to me.'

'But I can't help,' Christy protested. '*I* don't have any medical training.'

'I don't want you for that.' Dominic frowned as though in an indictment of her stupidity. 'I want you to take charge of her children. Her husband's out on the hills with his sheep, and she's got twins and a toddler, all under five. I'd ask your mother . . .'

'Mum and Dad aren't here. They've gone into Alnwick to see some friends.'

She wanted to protest that Dominic had no right to dragoon her into helping him like this, but her heart went out to the pregnant woman isolated from all the protection of modern medicine in her remote home, and somehow she found herself clambering into the Land Rover and holding her breath as Dominic put it into gear and the heavy four-wheel-drive vehicle inched slowly through the deepening snow.

It was a hair-raising journey to the farm—only four

miles away from her parents' house, but much, much higher in the hills and consequently even more exposed to the ferocity of the blizzard.

Three times the Land Rover got stuck and both she and Dominic had to get out and use the spades and grit he had packed in the back to get it moving again. Each time, as she wiped the freezing snow from her stinging face, Christy wondered what on earth she had let herself in for.

It seemed to take hours to reach the farm, and on the third occasion they became stuck she couldn't help asking Dominic uncertainly, 'Will she be all right . . . I mean . . .'

'She's a very sensible woman, and telephoned the surgery the moment she went into labour, knowing that it was going to be impossible for us to bring her down. Her baby wasn't due for another three weeks, and both the twins and her first child were late, so she wasn't prepared for this one's early arrival.'

Although he sounded calm, Christy could sense that Dominic was concerned and she shivered on a surge of sympathy and apprehension for the pregnant woman.

'Couldn't a helicopter . . . ?' she suggested timidly, but Dominic shook his head before she could finish her sentence.

'Nowhere for it to land; the house is on a fairly steep hillside. Look, I think you can see the lights from it up ahead.'

By straining her eyes Christy could just about make out the faint yellow gleam ahead of them. Staring into the snow made her eyes ache, and she marvelled at

Dominic's skill and stamina in managing to drive them this far.

She could hardly believe it when they finally rolled to a halt in the farmyard.

Two small tow-coloured heads poked round the back door as Christy jumped down from the Land Rover. The twins, no doubt, she decided, following Dominic inside. The kitchen was warmed by an immense Aga, the strain in the face of the woman sitting in front of it telling its own story.

'Sorry about the delay,' Dominic apologised. 'How are you feeling?'

Christy could almost feel for herself the spasm of pain that contorted the woman's body as she bent over.

It was several seconds before she could speak.

'I don't think it will be very much longer. I can't tell you how glad I am that you're here.' She saw Christy for the first time as she stepped out from behind Dominic and smiled wanly at her.

'I brought Christy to keep an eye on the children.' As Dominic spoke he was looking at his watch— timing the contractions, no doubt, Christy thought nervously. She had never had an awful lot to do with babies, and had certainly never been there on the spot, so to speak, when one was born.

'I've got everything ready upstairs, doctor.'

'All right, Mrs Thomson, I'll be with you in a minute. Can you cope down here?' Dominic asked Christy briskly, smiling reassuringly at the three small faces turned up to his with varying degrees of apprehension.

'Mummy's having our baby,' the largest member of the trio lisped.

'Yes . . . yes, I think so. Shouldn't I be boiling water or something?' Christy suggested distractedly.

Dominic laughed. 'No . . .'

It seemed a long, long time since she had heard him laughing naturally, and she could feel her own heart lifting slightly in response as she remembered earlier, more innocent days when she had been content with nothing more than his friendship.

Keeping the children occupied wasn't too hard a task. They were all obviously well-behaved, and the fact that she was a stranger further inhibited them, so that it wasn't until Christy had the brainwave of suggesting that they play Snakes and Ladders when she saw the game on the dresser that they started to relax a little.

Every now and again she glanced upwards, inwardly praying for the safety of Mrs Thomson and her baby.

When she cried out, the twins' faces puckered, and one of the little boys cuddled on to Christy's lap. Too young to really understand what was happening, they could still feel their mother's pain and react to it.

'Mummy cry . . .'

Christy watched despairingly as the small chin wobbled, but Lyn, the eldest of the three, came to her rescue, saying stalwartly, 'It's all right, Christopher . . . it's only like when Betsy had her puppies . . .'

That was one way of looking at it, Christy thought wryly, and of course as farm children they would be used to the actuality of birth.

Time seemed to drag as Christy waited in apprehensive silence. How long did it take for a baby to be born? She might as well have asked herself how long was a piece of string, she acknowledged ruefully. The problem was that she felt so woefully inadequate. She got up and checked on the Aga, going out for more fuel.

When she came back the twins asked for drinks, and with Lyn's help she found their orange juice. She had just got them settled when above them their mother cried out, the sound splintering the silence of the kitchen.

Christy held her breath, gathering the twins closer, and even the more stoical Lyn leaned tensely against her.

From the top of the stairs she heard Dominic calling her, and numbly she got up and hurried across the room.

'Can you come up here for a moment, Christy?'

He sounded calm enough, if a bit terse.

Gently reassuring the children and checking that the door was locked and there was nothing of any danger to them within their reach, she hurried upstairs.

Lorna Thomson's dark hair was clinging stickily to her face, and Christy felt a spasm of fear clutch at her stomach as she heard the other woman's moans.

'What is it?' she asked Dominic nervously, licking dry lips. 'Dominic, I . . .'

'It's all right. All I want you to do is to let Lorna hold on to you. Can you do that?'

The woman on the bed writhed and cried out, and

Christy forgot her fear.

'Soak a cloth in cold water, so that you can sponge her face,' Dominic instructed her.

As she sat at the side of the bed following Dominic's instructions and feeling the sharp bite of Lorna's fingernails into her skin, even Christy in her ignorance could see that the birth was imminent.

A huge wave of love and awe washed over her as she listened to Dominic exhorting and cajoling Lorna. She looked at him, watching the total concentration on his face, before she turned back to soothe Lorna's damp face.

'Just one more push, Lorna. You can do it. And another . . .'

Awed beyond belief, totally unable to look away, Christy witnessed the almost magical moment of birth. That the baby was scarlet and daubed with mucus and blood could not in any way detract from the wonder of what she had experienced, and if anyone had asked her what the baby looked like she knew she would have said, and meant it, 'Beautiful.'

Almost from a distance, she heard Dominic saying tiredly, 'Congratulations, Lorna, you have another daughter.'

From the side of the bed, Christy watched in wonderment as Dominic placed the tiny red-faced creature flat on her mother's stomach. There were tears in Lorna Thomson's eyes as she reached out to touch her new daughter's damp, dark head.

'Christy, why don't you go down and make us all a cup of tea?' Dominic suggested quietly, drawing her to one side, and pushing her gently in the direction of the door. For a moment she stood and watched him, knowing that she was completely forgotten as he went to attend to his patient.

Downstairs the children stared at her, round-eyed, and it was Lyn who asked, 'Has our new baby come yet?'

'Yes, she has,' Christy told them. 'Your mummy needs to have a sleep now, but as soon as she's rested, I expect you'll be able to go up and see her.'

'You're crying,' one of the twins accused, and as she touched trembling fingers to her damp face, Christy realised that she was. She felt privileged and elated in a way she couldn't explain to have witnessed the birth. It was something she would remember all her life.

Unwittingly she touched her own flat stomach and felt again that wave of desolation and failure that had encompassed her when she knew she wasn't going to have Dominic's child.

They stayed at the farmhouse until Lorna Thomson's husband returned home. The blizzard had stopped, and the wind was dying down. Jack Thomson thanked them with tears in his eyes for what they had done, and Christy felt guilty that he should have thanked her when she had done so very little. The children had seen their mother and new sister now, and already Lyn was telling the twins importantly that babies weren't to be poked with inquisitive little fingers.

It was dark by the time they left, the snow freezing already. Christy shuddered, dreading the hazardous return journey.

It took them almost an hour, crawling over the hard-packed frozen snow, and when eventually the turning to the lane came in sight, she tensed as she looked in vain for a spiral of smoke from the sitting-room fire's chimney.

Sensing her tension, Dominic looked across at her. 'What's wrong?'

'I think the sitting-room fire's gone out.'

His frown deepened. 'If it has the house will be like an icebox; these stone houses always are.'

'We do have central heating, you know,' Christy pointed out as he stopped the Land Rover in front of the house. She was sliding out of her seat as she spoke, but somehow he seemed to have anticipated her, and he was there to take the back door key from her frozen fingers and unlock the door for her.

As she followed him inside, Christy's heart sank. She didn't need anyone to tell her that the heating had gone off. The air was icy enough to make her shiver.

She saw that Dominic was squatting down in front of the boiler, and realised that he was looking for the pilot light.

'You'd better come back with me,' he told her brusquely as he stood up. 'If I leave you here you'll freeze.'

If he'd put into words how little he wanted her company, he couldn't have made it plainer, and before she could stop herself Christy heard herself saying nastily, 'Won't Amanda have something to say about that?'

His eyes went cold. She'd forgotten how disapproving and quelling he could be when he looked down his nose like that.

'What could she have to say?' he asked coldly. 'You're the daughter of some old friends, whom I can hardly leave to spend the night in a freezing cold house when the temperature's already way down below freezing and still dropping, when my home is less than half a mile away.'

'Maybe your central heating isn't working either,' Christy suggested childishly. What had she been hoping? That he would deny that Amanda had any right to question his actions?

'Very likely,' he agreed coolly. Too coolly for Christy's liking. 'However, unlike you, I took the precaution of making sure that all my fires were well banked down before I came out.'

'So would I have done as well,' Christy fired up immediately, 'if you hadn't practically dragged me off before I could do so.'

Suddenly his face split in a grin she remembered from earlier and far, far happier times. Crossly she glared at him while he teased, 'You always were a cussed little brat, Christy. It must be something to do with this red hair.' He pushed back the hood of her anorak as he spoke and gently tugged one of her curls.

Heat rushed through her body and she stepped back from him instantly.

His smile faded, his face shuttered and cold.

'You've got ten minutes to collect together anything that you might need. What time do you expect your parents back?'

'I've no idea. Originally they would have come home tonight, but Dad rang and said that they would stay over in view of the weather.'

'Umm, well, if you give me the number, I'll give them a ring and tell them where you are while you collect your stuff.'

This was the old big brother Dominic she remembered from her pre-teens. She wanted to protest that she was perfectly capable of looking after herself, but as she looked up her parents'· friends' telephone number, she was already starting to shiver in the chill air.

It didn't take her long to collect what she wanted, and while she was upstairs she would have liked to have changed out of her damp jeans and anorak—they had had to get out of the Land Rover twice on the way back to dig it out, and on both occasions the snow had come over the top of her wellington boots—but she didn't want to give Dominic any more excuse than necessary to criticise her, and criticise her he would if she kept him waiting, she thought bitterly.

If she was Amanda, he wouldn't be treating her so cavalierly. If she was Amanda. She punched the old velour dressing-gown she was shoving into her rollbag with unnecessary vigour and then grimaced to herself. If she was Amanda, no doubt she wouldn't be packing serviceable woollies and dressing-gown, but sheer silk undies and the sort of nightwear that no woman in her right mind ever wore to keep warm.

He was just replacing the receiver when she went back downstairs.

'Your parents *were* worried about you. Apparently they tried to ring this afternoon to check that you were all right. I've explained the situation to them and your mother said you weren't to worry, and that they would be back tomorrow after lunch.'

So she wasn't to worry, Christy thought grimly as she allowed Dominic to take her bag and then waited impatiently while he locked the back door. How was she supposed to feel, forced to spend the night with the man she loved, knowing how little he desired her? She only hoped that he gave her a bedroom with a lock on the door, so that she wasn't tempted to sleepwalk into his bedroom and betray herself completely.

'Oh, I'm not worried at all,' she assured him nastily, refusing to allow him to help her into the Land Rover, 'but Amanda might be if she knew that the two of us were spending the night together.'

He was right, she was behaving like an absolute brat, she thought guiltily, watching the angry flush of colour seep up under his skin. She only hoped that he wouldn't realise that it was sheer jealousy that was making her so objectionable.

'Spending the night together is hardly the way I would describe our situation.' He practically gritted the words through his teeth, throwing them over his shoulder at her as he started the engine. 'And even if we were, what possible reason could Amanda or anyone else have for objecting? We are both, after all, consenting adults, even if one of us isn't behaving like one.'

She had the grace to squirm a little uncomfortably on her seat. 'It's hardly my fault if everyone round here thinks of you and Amanda as an established couple,' she muttered.

One darkly raised eyebrow informed her that he suspected the truth had been subjected to some imaginative expansion.

'Don't talk rubbish, Christy. It might suit you to believe that I sublimated my need for Amanda in making love to you in the same way you sublimated yours for David Galvin, but you won't get me to swallow such an unappetising lump of fiction simply to soothe your conscience.'

'But you were *dating* her.' Why on earth was she being so stubbornly persistent? Dominic had turned out into the lane now and she could see his house up ahead of them in the glare of the headlights.

'Was I? You seem to know more about our relationship than I do,' he said drily. 'I thought we were simply thrown together by force of circumstances.'

'But you . . .'

On the point of reminding him that he had gone to London with the other girl, she suddenly realised what a dangerous path she was treading and closed her mouth firmly before she could endanger herself any further.

'Stop looking for excuses, Christy.' His voice was harsh, and edged with temper. 'What happened between us happened, and I for one don't regret it.'

He stopped the Land Rover with a jerk that made it slide forward a few feet, jolting Christy slightly against her seat belt. As she straightened her body she could feel her heart pounding like a steam engine.

'I'm tired of getting the cold-shoulder treatment. I'm sorry if I wasn't the man you wanted to take your virginity, more sorry than I can say.' He sounded tired now, and guiltily she realised what a strain the whole

afternoon must have been for him. 'If you want me to
apologise for making love to you, or to say that I regret
it, I'm afraid you're going to be disappointed.'

For the first time since she had known him, he
turned his back on her and got out of the Land Rover
without either waiting to help her or checking that she
was following him.

He had reached the door before she realised how
cold she was and managed to stumble after him.

He had switched on the hall light, and its harsh
glare illuminated the tension in his face. He seemed to
be waiting for her to say something, but what could
she say? That *she* didn't regret it either; that . . . but
no, she couldn't say that, otherwise he might think . . .

What? That she might welcome his lovemaking
again? That she might be agreeable to just that sort of
brief affair she knew would tear her apart?

'Dominic, can't we declare a truce—just for
tonight?'

He looked down at her for a long time, his eyes
glittering oddly between the black fringe of his lashes.
He was looking at her almost as though he resented
having to do so . . . almost as though . . . her stomach
lurched and she touched her tongue to her lips
nervously.

'For God's sake, don't do that. Aren't things bad
enough as they are, without you behaving like a
provocative . . .' He broke off and swore as he saw her
face, reaching for her, but it was too late, Christy was
already backing away from him and running out into
the freezing darkness, his words hammering relent-
lessly against her brain as past and present met and

merged, and she was once again that vulnerable seventeen-year-old who had gone to him with the gift of her love and her body, and had been rejected.

'Christy ...' She heard him call her name, but it scarcely penetrated the turmoil of her thoughts. The snow was too thick for her to run, but she stumbled on, not knowing where she was going, only that she had to escape.

When Dominic grabbed hold of her from behind, she cried out and turned to push him off, but her feet slipped and she fell backwards into the thick snow, taking Dominic with her.

His weight crushed the breath from her lungs, the cold sting of the snow on her face and the shocking awareness of losing her balance making her shiver convulsively beneath him.

'Christy—my God, are you all right?'

She had started to cry, huge, gulping sobs that tore at her throat until it was raw with pain from trying to drag in lungfuls of icy cold air. She could feel the warmth of her own tears on her face as Dominic levered himself up off her.

He picked her up, striding back to the house, carrying her into his study.

Oh God, if he had brought her to any room but this! Snow clung to her clothes, but he seemed unaware of it as he sat her in front of the fire and started to tug off her wellington boots.

'Christy, I'm sorry ... I'm sorry ... I didn't mean ...' His words were a husky, pleading sound that washed against her ears, without their meaning really penetrating. She shivered, protesting between sobs as he pulled off her socks and rubbed her freezing feet.

'Christy, listen to me ... It was just my vile, abominable temper. I never meant ...'

She heard him curse and the sound penetrated, her blank eyes focusing on his face.

'Come on. Let's get you out of these wet things.' He spoke to her as gently as though she was a child, and like a child she sat lethargically and let him strip her down to her underwear and then wrap her in a warm towel that he brought down from upstairs.

'You stay here. I'll go and make us both a hot drink.'

By the time he came back she had herself under control. When he came in with two mugs of coffee she said huskily, 'I'm sorry, that was a stupid thing to do.'

'We all do stupid things at times.' He looked so sombre and drawn that she yearned to cradle his head against her breast and comfort him.

'It was wonderful ... this afternoon,' she said half shyly, searching for a safe subject for conversation. 'So beautiful ... that perfect baby.'

Something in the yearning quality of her voice must have reached him because he said softly, 'Would *you* like children, Christy?'

Only yours. She flushed as she thought she had spoken out loud, gratefully realising that she hadn't after all.

'Yes ... yes, I would.'

His face darkened suddenly. He got up and stared down at her. 'It's no good, I promised myself I wouldn't interfere, but I can't stand by and see you ruin your life. Think of all that you're giving up by holding on to your love for David Galvin. *He* doesn't

love you to the same extent. Surely you must see that.
He'll never give you children, Christy. He already has
a wife and family.'

She looked at him, curiously warmed by the fire and
the coffee, wondering at the intensity in his voice.

'Have you ever been in love, Dominic?'

He frowned and turned away from her so that his
face was in the shadows. 'Yes . . .' He sounded terse.

'And . . . and did she love you too?' Why on earth
was she tormenting herself like this?

'Once I thought she did.' The words seemed to be
dragged out of his throat under fierce pressure. 'But
. . . but I was wrong.'

Some girl in the States, perhaps. Maybe that was
even the reason why he had come home, but she
couldn't probe any further; she didn't have the right,
and neither did she have the strength to sit there and
listen to Dominic telling her about the woman he
loved.

'I've got some reports to write up; do you mind if I
do some work?'

Christy shook her head, watching as he walked over
to his desk and sat down. Within seconds he seemed
totally absorbed in what he was doing, leaving her free
to look her fill at him.

He worked for about an hour, but she wasn't bored;
The crackle of the logs and the faint sounds from his
desk as he wrote, the fact that she was here with him—
all these things filled her with a pleasure that was
tinged with melancholy. She fell asleep while he was
still working, unaware of the fact that he had put down
his pen to come and look broodingly down at her. Her

towel had slipped, revealing the gleaming curve of her shoulder. As he bent to tuck the towel round her she woke up.

It was a shock to find him so close. 'Are you still working?'

'No, I've finished now.' A faint smile tugged at his mouth. 'You're not my patient—remember? Do you feel hungry? Shall I make us something to eat?'

She pulled a face and said drowsily, 'I seem to have lost my appetite recently.' For a moment he stared at her, and then he tensed.

'My God, Christy, you're not . . .'

As his hands gripped her shoulders she stared back at him and then suddenly realised what he thought.

'No . . . No, I'm not pregnant . . .'

It was ridiculous to think she had seen disappointment momentarily darken his eyes, and she told herself that seeing things that weren't there was a very dangerous symptom.

'When I said that about you being provocative, I didn't mean what you thought, you know,' Dominic said abruptly.

'You mean you weren't trying to remind me that there was a time when I had been guilty of being extremely provocative? No, I know you weren't, Dominic. I don't know why I ran off like that . . . it all got too much for me, I suppose.' She shivered intensely at the memory of her own folly.

'Cold?' Dominic's hands rubbed her arms through the towel. 'I'd better go upstairs and light a fire in one of the bedrooms for you, otherwise you'll freeze tonight.'

'Only one? What about you?' She felt hot at the stupidity of her unwary tongue.

To her relief Dominic seemed unaware of the ambiguity of her question. She had half expected him to make some taunting remark asking her if she was inviting him to share a room with her, but instead all he said was, 'Oh, I won't need one. I don't often feel the cold. I seem to be equipped with my own very efficient central heating. Your bag's in the hall. Do you want me to bring it in?'

She nodded her head. While he was lighting the fire she could put on some clothes. Although she hadn't said anything to Dominic, even her bra was soaked through after her tumble in the snow, and she was anxious to remove its cold clamminess from her skin.

She waited until she heard his feet on the stairs before slipping out of the towel and stripping off her damp bra, shivering a little, her skin still chilled.

She had only brought one change of underwear, so after a moment's hesitation, she pulled on a thick sweater, hoping that its bulkiness would disguise the fact that she wasn't wearing a bra underneath it.

The damp one she rolled up with her other discarded clothes and stuffed in one half of the rollbag before putting on a pleated woollen skirt of soft olive and yellow checks. The skirt buttoned up the back, and the thick sweater she was wearing was in the same olive as the check. It was an outfit she had had for quite a long time and she was surprised to see Dominic stand just inside the doorway for what seemed like a long time, simply looking at her.

'It's snowing again,' he told her.

'Will Lorna and the baby be all right?' She shivered as she remembered the cold drive to the remote farm.

'Yes, they'll be fine. Lorna's an experienced mother, don't forget, and people who live as close to nature as they do know all about protecting themselves from the elements. It's the city dwellers who can't cope. If there's a power cut they're marooned without light and heat in their multi-storey flats. The Thomsons have open fires and paraffin lanterns.'

Almost as though by some freak coincidence, as he spoke the light bulbs flickered and from outside came the sound of the wind. It flickered again twice, and then abruptly it was dark.

'That's all we need!'

'Have you got any lanterns?' Christy asked him wryly.

'There are probably some in the cellar, but I'm damned if I'm going to go down there and risk breaking my neck. We'll have to make do with candles.'

Candlelight and log fire, it was far, far too intimate, Christy acknowledged. She could almost feel her mind disintegrating and her senses taking over.

'Tell me about America?'

Dominic was sitting opposite her, and for a moment as he looked at her she thought he had guessed how his closeness affected her.

'There isn't much to tell,' he began, but nevertheless some of the stories he told her about his patients were amusing, and as she listened and laughed she forgot that shared laughter could be as dangerous as shared silence—perhaps even more so.

They ate supper—a casserole that Dominic had heated and served, refusing to let Christy do anything—and now as she sat with her fingers curled round a mug of chocolate she could feel a sleepy lethargy washing over her. She put down her mug and leaned back in her chair. She would just close her eyes for a few minutes . . .

Half an hour later she was still asleep. Dominic bent down to look at her and then picked her up. She stirred briefly in his arms, burying her head against him with a contented sound of pleasure. His arms tightened and he frowned.

Upstairs in the room he had prepared for her, firelight danced on the walls, highlighting the floral trellis pattern of the old-fashioned wallpaper.

He put her on the bed, and then threw more logs on the fire and walked back to her. He could hardly let her sleep in her clothes.

Christy woke up as he started to tug off her jumper, clutching it against herself protestingly.

'Christy, you can't go to bed in it. Come on. Look, I've got your night things here.'

Muzzy with sleep, she tried to remember why it was so important that Dominic didn't take off her jumper, but it was too much of an effort, and so she let him pull it off, only remembering why he shouldn't when she felt the cool rush of air against her naked breasts.

She saw him looking at her and felt the responsive quiver deep down in her stomach.

It wasn't a surprise when he moved to take her in his arms; part of her had been waiting for him to touch her all evening . . . had been waiting for it and wanting it.

Her lips clung softly to his, her skin delighting in the sensation of his hands moving hungrily against it.

She could feel his heart thumping and knew that her own echoed its frantic beat. There was need and hunger in the way that he kissed her, and she couldn't deny her own response to him.

'Christy, let me stay with you tonight.' The words were muffled against her skin as he tasted the creamy vulnerability of her throat. 'I want you so much.'

Ironically, if he hadn't spoken she would have gone with him to hell and back, but the raw, almost agonised sound of his voice had broken the delicate spell, and she moved away from him, shivering with too much tension and emotion.

'I can't.'

'Why not?' His voice was thick and tortured. 'Is it because of him?' His face contorted and she shuddered as she recognised the sexual jealousy glittering starkly in his eyes. 'You might love him, Christy, but you can't have him. And besides, you want me.'

His hand touched her breast to underline his meaning, the brief sensation of the pad of his thumb against the taut thrust of her nipple almost agonising.

'Be with me tonight . . .'

'No . . .' The denial was torn from her throat, making it ache. It was all too much; she couldn't go on pretending any longer. 'You don't understand, Dominic,' she told him wretchedly. 'I don't love David, I never have . . . Oh, he wanted me for a while, just as he's wanted a dozen or more women, and sexually he's very attractive, but I've never loved him.'

He looked at her hard, but she held his eyes until she saw that he believed her. If anything he seemed even more tense, and then he said rawly. 'If you don't love him, then why . . .'

She didn't let him go on. She was far too wrought up as it was.

'Can't you *guess*? I don't want to have sex with you, Dominic . . .'

She saw him flinch back from her feverish words. A dark tide of colour burned up under his skin, and he looked almost as wretched as she felt.

'I can't go to bed with you, Dominic; I can't involve myself in a brief affair with you, because it would tear me apart. I love you too much.'

There, it was said. He would leave her alone now. She turned away from him, waiting to hear the sound of the door closing behind him. Dominic had his own code of honour; now that he knew the truth he would understand, and so she waited, tense and frighteningly close to the edge of her self-control.

When he touched her she flinched almost as much as he had done earlier, but his grip compelled her to turn round and look at him.

'Let me get this straight.' He was speaking slowly, breathing heavily as though fighting to control a huge inner rage. 'You *won't* make love with me because *you love me*?'

For the first time in her life she was frightened of him. He wasn't reacting the way she had expected. He looked angry, violently, dangerously angry, and he was looking at her in a way that made her skin crawl with fear.

'Is that what you're saying?'

He shook her and she tensed beneath his hand. It was too late to lie now. 'Yes.'

He released her so unexpectedly that she fell back against the bed, watching him with nervous eyes. He was staring up at the ceiling, swallowing hard.

'I don't believe this.' His voice was flat and hard.

'Why do you think I made love with you in the first place?' Her voice was nowhere near as self-controlled as his had been. 'It certainly wasn't because of anything to do with David.'

'All these years I've fought against coming back ... told myself that what you felt for me was just an adolescent's emotion. I kept in touch with your parents, hoarding every little nugget of information I got from them. I thought you were happy in London— the career woman who put her job first and her lovers second. I tried every way I knew to forget you, and to stop myself from going mad because I'd fallen in love with a child of seventeen. Have you any idea what that does to a man? It made me feel like some sort of pervert. It got so bad that I couldn't trust myself alone with you. What in *God's* name made you think that all I wanted was a cheap affair?'

She was almost too stunned to speak.

'I ... You only said that you wanted me ... I thought it was just sex ... When I mentioned Amanda you said she was looking for a husband, and implied that you weren't interested.'

'Of course I damned well wasn't! There's only ever

been one woman I've wanted to marry, and that's you.'

He reached for her, dragging her into his arms, his voice muffled against her. 'Christy ... when I think how close we've just come to losing each other ... Tonight when you said you didn't want me ...' He broke of, gripping her tightly.

'I couldn't bear to make love with you. I was terrified of what I might reveal. Did you really love me all those years ago?' She couldn't believe it.

His smile was slightly crooked. 'Want me to show you how much?' He laughed softly at her expression. 'When you were seventeen I was twenty-five, plenty old enough to know what I wanted from life, and old enough to be terrified of the way I felt. One of the reasons I went to the States was that I felt I couldn't trust myself not to manipulate you into a relationship you weren't really ready for. It would have been all too easy to take advantage of your adolescent feelings for me and to persuade you into marriage, and I knew that wouldn't be right.'

His thumb stroked the softness of her lower lip and she caught it in her teeth, biting it gently, her eyes widening as she caught his harshly indrawn breath.

'The first thing I'm going to do when this snow lets us out of here is to get us a special licence,' he told her huskily.

It was her turn to laugh, a confident, happy sound, knowing that he loved her. 'And until then?' she teased.

'When I asked you this afternoon if you were pregnant, I was secretly hoping that you might be.

Then you would have *had* to marry me, or so I told myself, and I'm afraid a rather base male instinct still makes me feel that it would be a very good way of making sure that you can't run away from me.'

Dominic's child. Emotion quivered through her, and she held out her arms to him.

'Stay wth me tonight,' she whispered against his ear. 'We've already spent far too many nights apart.'

'Are you sure that this is really what you want?' She could see the tension in his eyes as he waited for her response.

'I'm sure.'

Christy moved her mouth to his, kissing him slowly, savouring the taste and texture of him.

Against the provocatively lazy movement of her lips he muttered, 'If you keep on doing that, you're going to get yourself in an awful lot of trouble.'

Suppressing the bubble of laughter welling up inside her, Christy reponded softly, 'Mmm, do you know, that was exactly what I had in mind.'

Coming in April
Harlequin Category Romance Specials!

Look for six new and exciting titles from this mix of two genres.

4 Regencies—lighthearted romances set in England's Regency period (1811-1820)

2 Gothics—romance plus suspense, drama and adventure

Regencies

Daughters Four by Dixie Lee McKeone
She set out to matchmake for her sister, but reckoned without the Earl of Beresford's devilish sense of humor.

Contrary Lovers by Clarice Peters
A secret marriage contract bound her to the most interfering man she'd ever met!

Miss Dalrymple's Virtue by Margaret Westhaven
She needed a wealthy patron—and set out to buy one with the only thing she had of value....

The Parson's Pleasure by Patricia Wynn
Fate was cruel, showing her the ideal man, then making it impossible for her to have him....

Gothics

Shadow over Bright Star by Irene M. Pascoe
Did he want her shares to the silver mine, her love—or her life?

Secret at Orient Point by Patricia Werner
They seemed destined for tragedy despite the attraction between them....

CAT88A-1

GIFTS FROM THE HEART

MAIL-IN-OFFER
OFFER CERTIFICATE ✂

I have enclosed the required number of proofs of purchase from any specially marked "Gifts From The Heart" Harlequin romance book, plus cash register receipts and a check or money order payable to Harlequin Gifts From The Heart Offer, to cover postage and handling.

002

CHECK ONE	ITEM	# OF PROOFS OF PURCHASE	POSTAGE & HANDLING FEE
	01 Brass Picture Frame	2	$ 1.00
	02 Heart-Shaped Candle Holders with Candles	3	$ 1.00
	03 Heart-Shaped Keepsake Box	4	$ 1.00
	04 Gold-Plated Heart Pendant	5	$ 1.00
	05 Collectors' Doll Limited quantities available	12	$ 2.75

NAME _____

STREET ADDRESS _____ APT. # _____

CITY _____ STATE _____ ZIP _____

Mail this certificate, designated number of proofs of purchase (inside back page) and check or money order for postage and handling to:

Gifts From The Heart, P.O. Box 4814
Reidsville, N. Carolina 27322-4814

NOTE THIS IMPORTANT OFFER'S TERMS

OFFER-1RR

GIFTS FROM THE HEART

from Harlequin

FREE BY MAIL

With proofs of purchase plus postage and handling

A. Hand-polished solid brass picture frame 1-5/8″ × 1-3/8″ with 2 proofs of purchase.

B. Individually handworked, pair of heart-shaped glass candle holders (2″ diameter), 6″ candles included, with 3 proofs of purchase.

C. Heart-shaped porcelain keepsake box (1″ high) with delicate flower motif with 4 proofs of purchase.

D. Radiant gold-plated heart pendant on 16″ chain with complimentary satin pouch with 5 proofs of purchase.

E. Beautiful collectors' doll with genuine porcelain face, hands and feet, and a charming heart appliqué on dress with 12 proofs of purchase. Limited quantities available. See offer terms.

HERE IS HOW TO GET YOUR FREE GIFTS

Send us the required number of proofs of purchase (below) of specially marked ''Gifts From The Heart'' Harlequin books and cash register receipts with the Offer Certificate (available in the back pages) properly completed, plus a check or money order (do not send cash) payable to Harlequin Gifts From The Heart Offer. We'll RUSH you your specified gift. Hurry—Limited quantities of collectors' doll available. See offer terms.

102R

GIFTS FROM THE HEART
ONE PROOF
OF PURCHASE

To collect your free gift by mail you must include the necessary number of proofs of purchase with order certificate.